The Earth Project

by Steven L. Stern

AMSCO

AMSCO SCHOOL PUBLICATIONS, INC.
315 Hudson Street / New York, N.Y. 10013

To Doron,
Better than a brother.

Text Design by Merrill Haber

Cover Design by A Good Thing, Inc.

Compositor and Artwork: A Good Thing, Inc.

Please visit our Web site at:

www.amscopub.com

When ordering this book, please specify:
either **R 697 P** *or*
THE EARTH PROJECT

Amsco Originals

ISBN 1-56765-068-6
NYC Item 56765-068-5

Printed in the United States of America

1 2 3 4 5 6 7 8 9 10   04 03 02 01 00

Chapter 1

The night sky hung over Jackson Field like a black sheet. A hundred stars twinkled in the darkness. A thin slice of moon cast a pale light.

The trees around the field rustled in the October breeze. Crickets filled the air with their song. Otherwise, the big field was silent and black.

Far above, a sudden spear of light flashed. A meteor streaked across the sky, burning white hot. Such "shooting stars" were common in the skies above the small town of Monroe.

But there was nothing common about this one.

The mass of rock sped through space. It was small, the size of a soccer ball. It moved straight toward Earth, falling hundreds of miles a minute.

And then something impossible happened. The meteorite's speed suddenly changed. The rock began to *slow*.

As it dropped, the meteorite glowed faintly. It was moving more and more slowly now. In fact, it seemed almost to be drifting down to Earth.

When it landed, the rock did not hit the ground like other meteorites. There was no crash. It scattered no dust. It carved no hole into the dirt. Instead, the brown rock touched down at the far end of Jackson Field with just a dull thud. Not like a meteorite at all.

"I'm glad it's Friday," Alicia said. She swung her backpack to the other shoulder as she walked.

Ryan didn't hear. He had other things on his mind.

"Can you believe it? Holly gave me a *C* on that paper. A *C*." He slapped at a low tree branch. "I was up half the night writing it." He shook his head. "My Dad's going to eat me alive."

Alicia took his arm. Why Ryan always waited until the last minute to do his papers she couldn't understand. He was smarter than that.

"Calm down, Ry. You'll probably still pull the B." Alicia wasn't really so sure that he would. Mrs. Holly was the toughest teacher in the school. Kids called her "Holly Heartless." But there was nothing Ryan could do about the paper now.

They walked along the road in silence for a while. Glen Lane wound its way past scattered small houses toward Jackson Field. After school on Fridays, many of the seniors hung out at "the Field." Kicking off the weekend this way had become a custom at Monroe High. Other afternoons, the Field was open to anyone. But Fridays it was seniors only.

"Hey! Wait up."

Tracy Mason trotted up beside them. She was short, with neatly cut black hair. Tracy was a straight-A student, one of the smartest kids in school. She was also one of the most annoying. Both her parents were lawyers. They used their legal fees to buy Tracy anything and everything she asked for. Tracy didn't appreciate what she had. But she always wanted more.

"It's Spacey Tracy," Ryan said. This was one of several nicknames the kids had given her.

"Don't call me that," she said, frowning.

"Hi, Tracy," Alicia said. Like Ryan, she didn't much care for the girl. But sometimes she felt sorry for her. Hard as she might try, Tracy was someone who'd never quite fit in. Her parents had done a royal job of screwing her up. But that wasn't Tracy's fault.

"Are you going to the Field?" Tracy asked.

"Looks like," Ryan said shortly. He was sure Tracy had never gotten a C in her life.

"Something bite your behind today?" Tracy asked.

"Holly didn't like his history paper," Alicia explained. She'd been dating Ryan Blake for five months now. She knew his moods. It would take Ryan a while to chill out.

"Oh, that. I got an A," Tracy announced." She

had a knack for saying exactly the wrong thing.

Ryan gave her a look. He started to say something, but Alicia squeezed his arm. There was no point to getting on Tracy. She was book-smart. But when it came to people, she was clueless.

They were almost at the Field now. Other teens joined them as they walked. Debra Barnes gave them a sunny hello. Debra had been Alicia's best friend since third grade. Alicia and Debra claimed to be twins. This was their joke. Alicia was white, and Debra was African American.

With Debra was Rachel Hoffman. Rachel was a talented violinist whose main interest was boys. Gina and Matt came next, arm in arm. The two had been a couple forever, or so it seemed. Right behind them was Nicolas Santiago. As always, he had on his purple baseball cap. Nick was known for his bad jokes and sweet tooth.

"Hey, Tracy," Nick said. "Nice sweater. Can I have it when you're done?"

Tracy's wardrobe was a legend at school. The word was that she had so many clothes that she never wore the same garment twice.

"I don't think green's your color, Nick," she said.

"Check me after a few beers."

"Nick's never had a beer in his life," Ryan said so only Alicia could hear.

She smiled. They both liked Nick.

As they walked onto Jackson Field, they greeted other students already there. Nearly thirty kids were spread about. Some sat on the grass. Others perched on the rocks. Most were eating junk food and talking over the day's events. One group was tossing around an orange Frisbee. Another group had moved to the shade of the trees, either to get out of the sun or to be alone.

It was ironic that Jackson Field had become a hangout for Monroe's teens. Sherman Jackson, who had owned the two-acre field until his death, had never had any children. In fact, he had never married. Instead, he spent all his time making real estate deals.

Jackson had died three years ago at the age of 91. He left the land to the town of Monroe, where he had grown up. In his will, Jackson asked the town to put the partly cleared field to good use. But the people of Monroe couldn't decide what that use should be. So, the land had remained untouched. Of course, a garbage truck did stop by twice a week to collect trash from the cans at the field's main entrance.

Alicia and Ryan flopped down on the grass. "Did you bring me something to eat?" Alicia asked. "I'm starving."

Ryan grinned. He was feeling better.

"Well, let's see . . ." He unzipped his backpack and held it open for her to see. "Would Madam care to dine?" Four cans of iced tea and a large bag of Oreos were jammed in with the books and papers.

"Oreos!" She gave him a hug. "I'm yours forever." She grabbed the bag.

"Did someone say Oreos?" Debra asked. She dropped down next to Alicia. Rachel, Nick, Gina, and Matt followed.

"Vultures," Alicia said.

By the time they'd finished the cookies, Jackson Field was one big party. Over forty teens were there now, with more coming. Kids were scattered everywhere. They were chatting, shouting, laughing, playing cards, wrestling in the grass, kissing under the trees. Boom boxes and CD players blasted the air. Some teens were dancing and singing. Zachary Smits—known as "El Wacko"—was racing around, trying to get a pink-and-green kite into the air. Kids clapped and cheered him on.

No one saw the slight movement at the far end of the field.

A brown rock began to vibrate softly. A crack at the top of the rock widened. Four thin metal rods rose from inside. The rods slowly turned. Each moved at its own speed, gathering data.

A half hour passed.

The rods vanished back inside the rock.

Two tiny, silvery disks appeared. Then three more. And another three. They all rose into the air.

The disks were smaller than pinheads. They were made of neither metal nor plastic. In fact, they were made of no substance found on Earth.

The tiny disks flew through the air like insects leaving a hive. They moved silently, invisibly.

One disk came to rest behind Tracy Mason's left ear. It gently fastened itself to her skin. Tracy felt nothing.

Another disk landed on Zachary Smits. It stuck itself to Zachary's neck, below the collar of his shirt. Zachary scratched the spot. Then he went on flying his kite.

One by one, each disk found a target.

The last disk attached itself to the skin under Ryan Blake's long black hair. Ryan, at that moment kissing Alicia, didn't notice.

Chapter 2

"Go slow, Alicia."

"I *am* going slow."

"Not slow enough," Debra said.

Alicia was behind the wheel of Debra's seven-year-old Oldsmobile. This was Alicia's third driving lesson with her friend. They were cruising Monroe's back roads. It was Thursday afternoon, and there was almost no traffic.

Alicia stepped down hard on the brake. Debra had to put out her hands to keep from hitting the dashboard.

"Go *easy!*"

"Why can't I do this?" Alicia said. She pushed her long brown hair away from her face. "This is so frustrating."

"You'll get it. Just takes practice." Debra smiled. "Parking is what will really make you nuts."

Alicia looked at her. "I can't wait."

A boy on a bike sailed past them. Alicia hit the brakes.

"Watch the road, girl."

"I am, I am." She tightened her grip on the wheel.

"Make a left here."

Alicia turned the corner and stepped on the gas. The car lurched forward. Debra was thrown back against the seat.

"Sorry," Alicia said.

"You sure do have a lead foot."

"A what?"

"A lead foot. You know—driving like you've got cement in your shoes."

"Is that any way to talk to your best student?"

"My *only* student." The car jerked forward again. "My only *car,* too," she added. "So go slow. It's starting to rain."

"Can we eat?"

"You hungry?"

Alicia shook her head. "No. I just want to stop driving."

"Why? Can't find the windshield wiper switch?"

"You are just *so* funny."

"Oh, fine. Let's go to the diner."

"French fries again?"

Debra grinned. "How'd you know?"

"What else do you ever eat?" Alicia pulled over to the side of the road. "*You* drive."

Debra laughed. "I was planning to."

Rosco's had few customers at 4:30. But the diner would soon fill up with the dinner crowd.

"Did you see Rachel today?" Alicia asked, biting into a sandwich. "I was looking for her."

"She went home after second period. Said she wasn't feeling well."

"Cramps?"

Debra drowned a French fry in ketchup. "No. Bad headache."

Alicia frowned. "Anything else?"

"What do you mean?

"Anything besides a headache?"

"You mean like fever or something?"

"Yeah."

"No. She just said she had a bad headache." Debra stopped chewing, looked at her friend. "Problem?"

"No. Just funny."

"Funny ha-ha, or funny strange?"

"Funny strange, I guess."

Debra speared another fry. "Why?"

"Yesterday, Gina was complaining about a headache. Tuesday, I heard Zachary say his head felt like it was going to explode."

Debra popped the fry into her mouth. "Zachary puts Tabasco sauce on everything he eats. His head *should* explode."

Alicia couldn't help smiling. "You may have a point."

"Anyway," Debra said. "What's the big deal?

So a few kids have headaches. Maybe there's a flu going around."

"You're right." Alicia took a bite out of her sandwich. "Just weird that nobody is really sick or anything. Just bad headaches."

Debra wiped ketchup from her mouth. "Probably stress. Or hormones."

"I suppose."

Alicia sipped her soda. She often wished she could be more like her friend. Alicia tended to worry about things that most people didn't give much thought to. Debra, on the other hand, rarely let anything bother her.

"You want to go to the party Saturday night?" Debra asked.

"At Peter's house? Sure. I like Peter."

"Me too. Now I just have to convince Reggie to come." Reggie was Debra's on-again, off-again boyfriend.

Alicia gave her a playful wink. "Just tell him I'll be there. Reggie and I have a thing going."

Debra chuckled. "I'm not worried. You're not his type."

"And why is that?"

"He only likes girls who can drive."

Alicia threw a napkin at her.

"Cold, Deb. Very cold."

Chapter 3

Rachel popped the two pills into her mouth. She washed them down with orange juice. Her mother turned away from the kitchen stove and came over. Mrs. Hoffman was short and thin, just like her daughter. Both had wavy black hair.

"Still got that headache?"

"Bad as ever," Rachel said. "Feels like my brain's too big for my head."

Mrs. Hoffman touched her daughter's cheek. "You don't feel warm. Did you take your temperature?"

Rachel nodded. "No temp."

"Your throat hurt?"

"No."

"Stomach okay?"

"Fine"

"What about—"

"Stop, Mom," she shouted. The questions were making her head hurt worse. "I'm fine. Just this crappy headache."

"Watch your language."

Rachel took a deep breath. She had to get away from her mother. "I'm going to lie down." She started to leave the kitchen.

"Dinner's almost ready. Your father will be home any minute."

"I'm not hungry."

Mrs. Hoffman frowned. "You've got to eat. Maybe you should take your temperature again."

"Mom! Stop! *Please.*" She went to her room and shut the door.

She lay down on the bed and closed her eyes. Her mother meant well. But sometimes she made her crazy.

The phone on the night table rang. This was Rachel's own line, which she paid for with her own hard-earned money. She groaned. Rachel was a popular girl. She had already gotten half a dozen calls since she'd gotten home. Talking to her friends usually made her happy. Today it just made her head hurt. She reached for the phone.

"Hello?"

"Rachel? How're you doing?"

She knew the voice at once. "Hi Alicia. I've been better."

"Are you sick?"

"No. Just need a new head."

"I don't remember you ever having to leave school. You never get sick. Not even a cold."

"First time for everything." Alicia was a close friend, but Rachel was in no mood to chat.

"James says hi." Alicia was trying to cheer her up. Blue-eyed, broad-shouldered James was the boy most on Rachel's mind these days.

"Alicia, I have to go. Sorry."

"Okay. You feel better."

"Thanks. Bye."

She put down the phone. She tried to think about James. But she couldn't focus her thoughts.

She heard the front door open. Her father was home from work. Most nights she'd greet him with a hug. Tonight, though, she couldn't move.

There was a quick knock at her door. "Rachel! Daddy's home. Dinner in ten minutes."

Rachel pulled the pillow over her face. The last thing she wanted to do was eat.

Somehow Rachel made it through dinner. Then she went straight to her room. She tried to do some math homework, but the numbers seemed to dance across the page. Finally, she gave up. Her headache was no worse. But it was no better either. She felt suddenly very tired. By 10:30, she was asleep. Her parents went to sleep an hour later.

The dreams began just before 1:00 A.M. At first, there were just pale colors. Reds and blues. Green. Orange. Yellow. Then the colors became shapes. They began to move, mix with one another. As they blended, they grew brighter.

And brighter. And brighter still. They became colored flames. The flames flashed and flickered in Rachel's brain.

Rachel's sleep became more and more restless. She turned over, threw off the sheet. "Colors . . ." she mumbled. She moved her hand to her eyes, trying to shield them. "Bright . . ."

Suddenly, she sat up in bed. Her eyes opened wide. She was neither awake nor asleep.

Have to go.

The words echoed in her brain.

Have to go.

The words drew her. Commanded her.

She slid out of the bed. She rose and went to her closet. She put on a pair of jeans, a sweater, sneakers. She moved slowly and silently.

Have to go.

She walked to the front door, unlocked it. She stepped out into the cool night air. The street was dark and quiet.

"*Have to go,*" she whispered and started walking.

Chapter 4

Ryan turned his blue Ford onto Elm Road. He found Peter's house and took the first open parking space. Many other cars already lined the street.

Alicia, Debra, and Reggie climbed out of the car. They were all in a great mood. Debra and Reggie held hands as they walked. Alicia was glad to see the two of them together again. They looked like a matched set, both of them tall and slim.

The party was in full swing when they walked in. Talking and laughing kids filled two rooms on the first floor. A third room was set aside for dancing. The music was so loud, it was hard to talk. Tables overflowed with food. There were cold cuts, rolls, salads, chips, and dips. Coolers were packed with soft drinks. One table contained all the fixings for tacos. Another was covered with cakes and cookies.

"Cool spread, Peter," Alicia said to the host. He had deep blue eyes set in a handsome baby face. Girls loved him. Alicia liked a more rugged look herself.

"Thanks. My parents cut loose at the market."

"Where are they?" Ryan asked.

"Hiding upstairs." Peter said. "I'm sure they'll drop in at some point."

"To look for beer?" Reggie said with a smile. His voice was surprisingly deep.

Peter gave him a look. "Get real." Peter had been caught drinking once. His parents had grounded him for a month.

"Let's dance, Reg," Debra said. Reggie grabbed a handful of chips and followed Debra into the other room.

Peter and Ryan began talking about sports. Alicia left them alone. She liked to play sports, not talk about them. She played soccer. She played basketball. She'd even been on the swim team. But chattering about players and teams bored her. And TV sports put her to sleep. She was a doer, not a watcher. Ryan and his friends could watch their games. Alicia would rather ride her bike.

She popped open a can of soda and made the rounds. She knew nearly everyone at the party. She was laughing at one of Nick Santiago's jokes when she saw Rachel. She excused herself and walked over.

"Rachel, how are you?" She almost had to shout to make herself heard over the music. "I wondered if you were going to make it." Rachel hadn't been in school Friday. Alicia hadn't spoken with her since their phone call on Thursday.

"Better," she said. "Headache's gone. I'm still pretty tired. My mom made me stay home an extra day to rest."

"So what was it? Some 24-hour bug?" Rachel looked fine, Alicia thought. A little pale, but otherwise okay.

"Yeah, I guess." Rachel hesitated. "It was scary, though."

"What was?" Alicia asked.

"I never get headaches. And . . ." She paused.

"And what?"

"Oh nothing. You'll think I'm a nut case."

Alicia laughed. "You *are* a nut case."

Rachel glanced around. "Let's go outside a sec. It's too hard to talk in here."

They moved out onto the porch. Four or five kids were there talking.

"Don't laugh, okay?" Rachel said. She stepped away from the other kids.

"What is it, Rach?" Alicia wondered what was on her friend's mind. When Rachel got serious, it usually meant she wanted to talk about boys.

"That night . . ." Her face clouded. "I think I must have been sleepwalking or something."

"What do you mean?"

"Maybe I was delirious."

"Rachel, what are you talking about?"

"Well . . . my head was killing me. So I went to bed early. And . . ." She paused again.

"And what?" Alicia said, giving her friend's arm a squeeze. Sometimes Rachel took forever to get to the point.

"Well, I woke up at about 5:30 in the morning." Rachel ran a hand through her wavy hair. "And . . . I wasn't in bed anymore."

"You weren't in bed? Where were you?"

Rachel looked embarrassed. "On . . . my front steps." She lowered her voice. "And I was dressed . . . . Weird, huh?"

"You don't remember going out?"

"I don't even remember getting up."

Alicia thought about this. She didn't know much about sleepwalking. But she supposed someone could pull on some clothes and wander downstairs.

"Something else," Rachel said. It was a relief to talk to Alicia. She hadn't told anyone else. Most of her friends would probably just laugh and tease her. She knew Alicia would listen.

"What?"

"This is just between us, okay?"

"Sure."

"There was mud on my sneakers."

"Mud?"

Rachel nodded.

"Mud from where?" Alicia asked.

"I have no clue."

Alicia didn't know what to make of this. "Did you tell your parents?" she asked.

"No way. They'd cart me off to a doctor. You

know how they are. Thank goodness they were still asleep when I went back inside."

Alicia thought for a moment.

"How did you feel yesterday?" she asked.

Rachel shrugged. "Okay. Tired. A little foggy. But no big deal."

"And last night? No problems?"

"Nope. I slept fine." She smiled. "And I woke up in my bed."

"By yourself?" Alicia asked, trying to lighten things up.

"Cute."

They fell silent.

"Well, it is strange," Alicia finally said. She was serious again. "But if you feel okay now, maybe it was just a one-time thing. Like a virus."

"That's what I figured."

"But if it happens again, you should proba-bly—"

"Yeah, I know. Go to the doctor. You sound like my mother."

They both laughed. Then Rachel leaned closer.

"Promise you won't say anything to anybody, okay?"

Alicia gave her a smile. "About what?"

By 1:00 A.M. the party was winding down. Peter's parents began to clean up. Some kids helped. Others were still eating.

Alicia and Ryan were strolling along Elm

Road. They had gone outside for a walk a half hour before. It was a cool night. Many stars dotted the sky. The quiet of the street was a relief after hours of music and talk.

They'd been walking with their arms around each other. Alicia kept her hand tucked in the back pocket of Ryan's jeans. It was a habit.

"Checking out my butt?" he once teased her.

"Checking out your brain," she'd answered, and they'd laughed.

They felt close, peaceful, tonight. At times like this, Alicia wondered if Ryan might turn out to be more than just "another boy."

There had been many. Alicia had started dating at 13. She was 17 now. She had liked many boys, but never loved one. Not really.

Sure, she'd thought she'd been in love a few times. She'd moon around the house. She'd doodle the boy's name in her notebook. She'd spend hours on the phone talking to him. And hours more talking *about* him.

But those had been crushes. If she was honest with herself, she didn't think she'd ever truly been in love. A part of her always held back.

She knew why. Alicia understood herself better than most kids her age. Two years with a shrink had seen to that.

She'd started seeing the shrink when she was nine. Right after her father died. It had been the worst time of her young life. Even now her insides burned when she thought about it.

There had been no warning. No chance for a good-bye. Nothing.

He'd left the house for work, as he did every day. And he'd just never come home again.

Heart attack.

Alicia had heard the words before. But she'd never thought much about them.

At age nine, she learned what they meant. They meant she'd never see her dad alive again.

At the funeral, everyone said the same things over and over.

"He was so young. . . just 44. Such a shame."

That poor woman. And her daughter . . . it's so unfair."

"Poor Alicia."

Poor Alicia. She had hated that. She didn't want to be "poor Alicia." She wanted to be just Alicia again. And she wanted her Daddy back.

In the years that followed, there had been many boys. Two or three had even said they loved her. Alicia had cared for some of them. Cared for, but not loved.

Don't feel too much, a voice inside her seemed to say. *People you love can disappear. They can disappear and never come back.*

Alicia cared for Ryan. More than most boys she'd dated. Ryan was smart. Sexy. Fun. Thoughtful. Warm. A little moody, but who wasn't?

Yes, she cared for him. Cared for him a lot. But love him? No way.

As they neared Peter's house, Ryan slowed. He was enjoying the night and didn't want it to end.

"You got quiet," he said. "You okay?"

"Sure. Just thinking."

He grinned. "About my good looks?"

"What good looks? You're a beast."

He stopped and faced her. Their eyes locked.

"Kiss the beast," he said softly.

They held each other close. The kiss lasted a long time.

They walked slowly the rest of the way to Peter's house.

Debra and Reggie were sitting on the front steps.

"It's about time," Debra said. "I was going to call a taxi." She wasn't mad. She just wanted to give them a hard time.

"Where did you two walk to?" Reggie said. "Cleveland?"

"What's your hurry?" Ryan asked.

"We figured you'd want to stay till the food ran out," Alicia said.

They all went inside to say their good-byes. Then they headed back to Ryan's car.

"That was fun." Debra said, as Ryan started the engine.

"I am so stuffed," Reggie said.

"You should have come for a walk, Ryan said. "Instead of sitting there like a lump."

"Hey, I got my exercise dancing, man." Reggie said.

"I didn't see you dance," Alicia teased. "Did he dance, Deb?"

"Nope. Just stuffed his face," Debra said. Reggie gave her a poke.

"Speaking of lumps, did Gina and Matt ever get up off that couch?" Alicia asked.

Everyone laughed. Gina and Matt had spent most of the night in their own little world. This happened often.

"Well, I know Gina went to the bathroom," Debra said. "I met her coming out. Told me another one of her wild stories." She chuckled. "I really do hope Matt marries her. That girl needs someone to keep an eye on her."

They drove down Elm Road and turned right onto Birch Street.

"Matt could use watching himself," Ryan said. "He's none too tightly wrapped."

Everyone laughed again. Most kids thought Gina and Matt were perfect together. Both were pleasant, quiet, and not too bright. And both were a little odd. Who but Gina and Matt would come to school in matching red sneakers?

"What was the story?" Alicia asked.

Debra rolled her eyes. "Oh, you know Gina. Stuff's always happening to her. Bat flying into her bedroom. Soup can exploding. Getting drunk and dropping her keys in the toilet."

"Don't forget the toaster fire," Reggie added.

Alicia started laughing. "I forgot about that."

"What happened?" Debra asked.

24

"Gina tried to make a grilled cheese sandwich in the toaster."

"She didn't."

"She did."

Laughter filled the car.

"So what was it this time?" Ryan asked. He slowed the car for a stop sign. "Little green men in her closet?"

"No, this time . . ." Debra was still laughing. She had to catch her breath. "This time she was sitting behind the wheel of her father's car. It's 6:00 A.M. She's wearing a T-shirt, shorts, shoes . . . and no underwear. The car's in the driveway. Motor's running."

"Where was she going?" Reggie asked.

"Or, coming from?" Alicia asked.

Ryan laughed. "That Matt. Watch those quiet guys."

"No, no." Debra shook her head, giggling. "Matt wasn't even there. Gina was home."

Reggie frowned. "I don't get it. What was she doing?"

"She has no idea," Debra said. She wiped a laugh tear from her eye. "Gina doesn't even know if she was coming or going."

"What else is new?" Ryan said. Everyone laughed.

"No, really. Gina says she went to bed with a bad headache. Next thing she knows, *poof!* She's sitting in the car." Debra began laughing again. "Do you believe that girl?"

"That's our little Gina," Ryan said.

"A real space case," Reggie said.

"Gina has no idea how she got there?" Alicia asked quietly. All of a sudden, this story didn't seem so funny.

"Zero," Debra said. "She doesn't even remember getting out of bed."

Alicia fell silent.

You don't remember going out? she had asked Rachel earlier.

I don't even remember getting up, Rachel had said.

Alicia wanted to say something. But she had promised Rachel not to.

"Did her folks catch her?" Reggie asked.

"No. They were asleep. Lucky thing."

"Probably wouldn't have mattered," Ryan said. He stopped the car in front of Debra's house.

"Why's that?" Debra asked.

"With Gina, they're probably used to strange."

Debra and Reggie laughed.

Alicia wasn't listening.

She doesn't even remember getting out of bed.

Maybe Rachel and Gina had the same 24-hour bug, Alicia thought. Anything was possible. But it was like no bug she'd ever heard of.

Chapter 5

"Oh, no, Mom. Tell me you didn't."

"Alicia—"

"Not Tracy."

"Don't get excited," Mrs. Lyons said. "It's just—"

"Don't get excited?" Alicia dropped her toast on the plate. It was 10:30 Sunday morning. She had slept late, but was still tired. "Do you *know* what Tracy's like? Do you know what her *parents* are like?"

"Mrs. Mason is a nice woman who was just trying to hel—"

"Mrs. Mason is worse than Tracy."

"That's harsh. Tracy has always seemed nice to me, and I—"

"Oh, stop saying how nice everyone is. That whole family is clueless. They think money is the answer to everything."

Mrs. Lyons sighed. She was an attractive woman who wore little makeup. Her hair was brown like her daughter's, but shorter.

"Alicia, I'm sorry. I didn't know what else to tell her."

You could have kept your mouth shut, Alicia thought. But she would never talk that way to her mother.

"You should have come up with an excuse."

"Listen, Alicia . . ." Mrs. Lyons hung up the dish towel and came to the table. She had expected this blowup.

Tomorrow afternoon, Mrs. Lyons was flying to Florida. Her 72-year-old mother had hurt her hip in a fall. Mrs. Lyons planned to spend a week with her. Maybe two. Luckily, she had plenty of vacation time due her at work.

Alicia would have to care for herself. This was not a problem. Alicia had stayed alone before. She'd had no choice. Mrs. Lyons was a single parent. She'd never had much money for baby-sitters. Sometimes she had to work late. Two or three times a year, she had to go on business trips.

Alicia often stayed with friends, but sometimes she wanted to stay alone. At first this made her mother uneasy. But the older her daughter got, the less Mrs. Lyons worried. Besides, neighbors were always ready to help.

Mrs. Lyons knew that Alicia had to grow up quickly after her father died. Too quickly, maybe. But she and her daughter had drawn strength from each other. They'd had to.

Mrs. Lyons sat down at the table across from

Alicia.

"Look, let me explain. I met Mrs. Mason at the store. We got to talking. I mentioned that I was going to Grandma's. I didn't think she was going to invite you. After all, you and Tracy have never been close."

"For sure."

"Anyway, for whatever reason, Mrs. Mason said you should stay with them. I thought it was a kind gesture."

"Charming."

"Don't be sarcastic."

Alicia silently sipped her orange juice. She didn't like to fight with her mother.

"At first, she said you should come for the week."

Alicia nearly spit up her juice.

"Relax. I tried to get out of it. But I didn't want to be rude. So I said you were very busy. But you'd be happy to spend a night or two. I'm sure if you sleep over one night, that will be fine."

"Fine for who?"

Mrs. Lyons frowned. "Enough, Alicia. You're overreacting. Anyway, I said I was sorry."

Alicia looked into her mother's eyes. They were clear and brown, like her own. But her mother looked tired. She worked long hours. She was worried about Grandma's hip. She didn't need more grief from her daughter.

"Forget it, Mom. No big thing." Alicia picked up her toast, took a bite. "You're right. I am overreacting. Tracy's not so bad."

Mrs. Lyons smiled at her.

"Thank you. You mean it?"

Alicia smiled back.

"No."

They both laughed.

Chapter 6

"You're staying at Tracy's house?" Ryan was surprised.

"Just for one night," Alicia said. It was
Tuesday afternoon. She and Ryan were sitting
on a bench behind the high school. School was
over, and kids were hanging out.

"Why?"

Alicia explained.

"So when is this pajama party?" he teased.

"Tonight. I thought I'd do it sooner rather
than later. I'm meeting Tracy at 5:30."

"And when do *I* get to sleep over?" He was
smiling. But Alicia knew he meant it.

"You mean at Tracy's house? I'll ask her for you."

"Very funny."

Alicia smiled back. He was so good-looking,
she thought. She loved that long black hair,
those dark eyes. The way the sides of his mouth
curled up when he grinned.

She remembered the last time they had her
house to themselves. Her mother was away on

business. They had been on the couch, watching TV. They had begun kissing. Then his hands were moving, touching her. The feeling was electric. It got better and better. She wanted it to last forever.

But she stopped him. Stopped him before things went too far. Stopped him as she always had before.

"Alicia—" He was breathing hard.

"No, Ry."

"Just . . . let's . . ."

"*No*, Ryan." She kissed him, then said the words again more softly. "No, Ryan."

He stopped. He didn't try to force her. He didn't try to convince her. He didn't pout, as some boys did. He just held her. And that meant more to Alicia than Ryan could know.

Sitting with him now, she wondered how many more times she would stop him. She sighed. Sometimes life was complicated.

"So, are you going to answer my question?" Ryan asked.

She smiled. "Are you busy this weekend?"

"Thanks for picking me up, Tracy." Alicia slid into the shiny black Mazda. She threw her bag into the backseat.

"No problem." Tracy put the car in gear. She pulled away from Alicia's house. "When are you getting your license?"

Alicia laughed. "When I can pass the road test."

"Have you been practicing?"

"Debra's been taking me out."

"How's it going?"

"I may have to buy a horse."

Tracy took them across town and up Breen Hill. This was Monroe's most expensive neighborhood. The houses were large. Every lawn was perfect.

They pulled into the long driveway of a stately gray home with black shutters. Shrubs and trees lined the huge front yard. Tracy left the car outside the two-car garage.

Alicia couldn't remember the last time she'd been at the Mason home. Two or three years, she guessed. She and Tracy had known each other since eighth grade. But they saw each other only at school.

The two girls ran in different circles. Alicia was into music, writing, and sports. Tracy hung out with the chemistry club and the debating team. Kids thought Alicia was cool and fun. They saw Tracy as dull, irritating, too smart, and too rich.

Tracy led the way through the large front hallway. The house was quiet.

"Nobody home?" Alicia asked.

"Are you joking? If either of my parents ever got home before 7:00, I'd faint. Don't worry. We won't wait dinner for them. I mostly eat before they get here anyway."

"You eat alone?"

She nodded. "Before my brother left for college, we'd sometimes eat together. Now I usually fend for myself."

Alicia thought about this. Her mom wasn't a big-deal lawyer like Tracy's parents. But she had a good job at a publishing company. Most nights she was home by 6:00. And she always insisted they eat dinner together. Alicia looked forward to it.

"You miss your brother?" Alicia asked. She'd always wanted a brother or a sister. But her mother hadn't been able to get pregnant again.

"Sometimes," Tracy said. "Mostly not. He's a pain. Besides, my pal Mac keeps me company."

"Who?"

She laughed. "Come on. I'll show you."

They walked into the kitchen. It was large and modern. The floor was white tile. There was a computer on the table. Alicia gave Tracy a puzzled look.

"This is Mac. Short for Macintosh," Tracy explained. "I'm on-line a lot. I can eat and chat with people all over the world." She giggled. "And I can talk with my mouth full."

"First time I've seen a computer in a kitchen," Alicia said. She had saved for a year to buy her own computer. She would never put it in the kitchen. She'd be too afraid of what spilled drinks and oven heat could do to the machine.

"We have four computers in this house," Tracy said. "Or is it five? I can't remember."

34

"You're lucky," Alicia said. But she wasn't so sure.

Alicia finished brushing her teeth. She walked down the second floor hallway to Tracy's room. Oil paintings hung on the walls.

She could hear Mr. Mason on the phone downstairs. Another business call. He spent a lot of time on the phone, Alicia thought. So did Tracy's mother. Alicia wondered if all the Masons were ever in the same room at the same time.

Tracy was already in bed. She had set up a cot for Alicia. The house had several empty rooms. But Tracy thought it would be fun for them to sleep in the same room.

"Tired?" Alicia asked.

"Yes. And I have a headache, which seems to be getting worse."

Alicia frowned. "Something's going around."

They talked for a while with the lights out. They had little in common besides school. Still, the evening had gone by quickly. Tracy was easier to be with than Alicia had expected.

Tracy had gone places and done things that most kids in Monroe couldn't afford. Alicia enjoyed hearing about them. To a point, at least. Sure, she felt a little jealous. Who wouldn't? Tracy had gone sailing in Hawaii. She'd skied in Switzerland. She didn't exactly brag about these things. She just took them for granted.

That's what many kids resented. Not that Tracy had so much. But that she acted as though none of it mattered. And maybe, Alicia thought, it didn't.

By midnight, the Mason house was silent. Once they'd stopped talking, Tracy had quickly fallen asleep. It took Alicia longer. She lay awake listening to Tracy's breathing. Once or twice, Tracy mumbled in her sleep. But Alicia couldn't understand the words. Finally, Alicia drifted off.

It was the closet door that woke her. It made a loud *click* when Tracy shut it.

Alicia rose on one elbow. She glanced at the clock radio on the night table. The red numbers glowed 1:28. She rubbed her eyes.

"What's up, Tracy?" she whispered.

The only light in the room came from a small night light. Alicia could see Tracy pulling a sweatshirt over her head.

"What's up?" Alicia repeated, yawning.

Tracy didn't answer.

"Are you okay?" Alicia kept her voice low. The Masons' bedroom was at the other end of the hall. But she didn't want to chance waking them.

No reply. Tracy put on a pair of pants.

Alicia sat up. "Tracy? Hello? Earth calling Tracy. Anybody home?"

Tracy didn't seem to hear her. She just kept getting dressed, staring straight ahead.

Alicia got up and moved closer.

"Tracy? Can you hear me?"

Tracy sat down on the edge of her bed. She pulled on a shoe.

Alicia didn't know what to do. What was it Rachel had said the other night? Something about sleepwalking?

Tracy pulled on the other shoe. She began to tie the laces.

Alicia's mind raced. Wasn't it dangerous to wake up a sleepwalker? She had read that somewhere once.

Tracy started on the laces of the other shoe. Her eyes were open. But she seemed to be staring at nothing.

Should I try to wake her? Should I get her parents? Alicia couldn't decide.

Tracy rose from the bed. She headed for the bedroom door.

"Tracy?" Alicia tried again.

Tracy opened the door.

"Tracy! Wait!"

She kept walking.

Alicia grabbed for her own clothes. She found her shirt. Her bra. Jeans. One sneaker. Where was the other one? She could hear Tracy start down the stairs. *Where was that other sneaker?*

There. Under the chair.

Alicia took off her night shirt and got dressed as fast as she could. She couldn't hear Tracy's steps. Most of the house was carpeted.

She tied her sneakers, snatched her jacket, and rushed out the door.

Down the stairs.

"Tracy?" she whispered at the foot of the stairs.

No answer.

She switched on a lamp, looked around.

"Tracy?"

She looked in the kitchen. Empty.

She checked the living room.

The den.

The bathroom.

No Tracy.

Alicia's heart thumped in her chest.

Where did she go?

And then she saw the open door. The door that led to the rec room.

And out to the garage.

Oh no!

Chapter 7

Alicia ran through the door. The rec room light was on. But no Tracy.

A car engine started.

Can't be, Alicia thought.

She dashed out to the garage. Through the open garage door, she could see the Mazda in the driveway.

Tracy was inside. Behind the wheel. She was shifting into gear.

"Tracy! No!"

Tracy started to back up.

Alicia ran to the passenger side. She yanked the door open and jumped in.

Tracy did not react. She kept backing up. Then she turned the car and headed out the driveway.

Alicia's heart was pounding. She watched Tracy, not sure what to do. She was afraid to grab the wheel, afraid not to.

Tracy slowly drove down Breen Hill. She seemed in total control of the car.

"Tracy, if this is a joke, it's not funny." Alicia's voice was hoarse. She knew it was no joke.

Tracy kept driving. Not too slow. Not too fast. Her eyes were fixed on the road. Her face was blank.

She's like a zombie, Alicia thought. *Or someone in a trance.*

She remembered a performer she'd once seen. The Amazing Quinn, he called himself. A gray-haired man in a black suit. Quinn took people from the audience. He hypnotized them. They seemed fine. They could walk and talk with no problem. But Quinn had them under his "spell." He made them do silly things. Bark like a dog. Dance with a broom. Sing songs. Laugh or cry. Afterwards, none of them remembered any of it.

She wondered what Quinn would say about Tracy.

They passed the grade school, the ball field, the old water tower. The roads were dimly lit, empty. There was no traffic in Monroe at this hour.

Despite her fear, Alicia found herself slowly getting calmer. Tracy seemed to know exactly where she was going. And she drove the car as well as ever.

Better than I drive, Alicia thought. The irony almost made her smile.

Tracy turned right on Old Hills Road. Her expression never changed. She kept her eyes on the road.

She's heading for the high school, Alicia thought. But when they reached the school, Tracy kept going.

"Where are you driving?" Alicia asked softly.

She didn't answer. Alicia hadn't really thought she would.

Tracy turned left onto Glen Lane. The road was a dead end.

"Jackson Field?" Alicia said, surprised. "Why are we going there?"

Tracy stopped near a street lamp at the main entrance. She turned off the engine and got out of the car. She started toward the field.

"Tracy?" Alicia slid out of the car. "Where are you going?"

Alicia looked out toward the big field. Beyond the street lamp, the only light came from the moon.

"Tracy," she called after her. "It's pitch black out there."

Tracy was already past the entrance.

"Tracy!"

She kept walking.

What do I do now? Alicia asked herself.

She didn't want to follow Tracy into the darkness. But she couldn't just let her walk away. The girl could break her neck out there in the dark.

Alicia leaned into the Mazda. She opened the glove compartment. She started pulling out the contents, searching.

"*Yes!*"

It was only a small flashlight. But it was better than nothing.

Alicia clicked it on.

She started after Tracy.

Chapter 8

Alicia moved the flashlight from side to side. The field was so dark that the thin beam of light was not much help.

She had to walk slowly. The ground was uneven. There were many rocks. Even with the flashlight, Alicia tripped several times.

"Tracy?"

No reply.

She kept walking even though she couldn't see the other girl. She wasn't even sure that she was still heading in the right direction.

"Tracy?"

Every few minutes she stopped. She swung the light around. She listened.

Crickets.

Crickets and silence.

The dark field was spooky. Alicia imagined animals lurking in the blackness.

Raccoons. Skunks.

Snakes. Foxes.

Bears.

Stop it, she told herself.

"Tracy?" she tried again, though she knew there was no point.

Crack.

The sound of the twig snapping came from some distance ahead. Alicia squinted into the darkness. Was that a figure she saw moving? She wasn't sure.

Another crack, farther away.

Alicia kept walking in the direction of the sound.

There. Way ahead of her, off to the left. A shadow moving. She was sure of it.

Alicia quickened her pace. Almost immediately she tripped over a branch. She banged her knee on a rock as she fell.

"Watch where you're walking," she scolded herself. She rubbed her knee. She started to rise to her feet, shaking her head. "I must be out of my min—"

A flash of light burst through the darkness. Alicia was so startled that she fell back to the ground. For a few seconds, she was blinded.

And then, maybe 70 yards ahead her, she saw Tracy.

Her short figure was outlined against an area of bright light. The area had an almost rectangular shape, like a doorway. The light seemed to shine up from the ground.

Alicia was too stunned to move. She just stayed on the ground, staring.

Tracy walked forward, into the light.
And then she was gone.
A moment later, the light went out.
Jackson Field was dark once more.

Chapter 9

For a few seconds, Alicia didn't move. She sat on the ground feeling numb. Slowly, her eyes adjusted to the dark again.

It had happened so fast. One minute Tracy was there. The next minute she was gone.

But gone where?

Alicia tried to understand what she had seen. She played the scene over and over again in her mind. The rectangle of light. Tracy vanishing. But she couldn't make any sense of it. She couldn't even come up with a theory.

Maybe I imagined the whole thing . . .

But where's Tracy?

She stared into the darkness, listening for any sounds. She heard only the crickets.

If this is a dream, please let me wake up now.

She got to her feet. Her legs felt shaky. Her knee hurt. Luckily, she hadn't lost the flashlight when she'd fallen. She couldn't imagine trying to walk back with no light at all.

But how could she go back without Tracy?

Well, Mr. and Mrs. Mason, here's what happened. Tracy got up in the middle of the night. She was in a trance. She drove to the Field. Then she disappeared into a bright light.

Yeah, right. Tracy's parents would really believe that.

They'd probably have her committed. Committed or arrested.

And who could blame them? Alicia thought. I don't believe what just happened.

Alicia stood there, not sure what to do. She thought about looking for Tracy. But how could she search for the girl in the dark?

The girl who had just vanished into thin air, she reminded herself.

How many hours were left before dawn? she wondered. Maybe in daylight she could find . . . find something . . .

Crack.

Something moving nearby. Something invisible in the blackness. An animal?

Alicia raised the flashlight. She stared into the dark. Suddenly, she felt afraid. Up until this moment, she had been thinking about Tracy. Now, for the first time, she feared for her own safety.

Alicia turned and headed back toward the car. She kept the flashlight pointed down at the ground ahead of her. She walked as fast as the thin beam of light would let her. She hoped nothing was following her.

After a few minutes, she could make out the dim light of the street lamp at the entrance. She kept walking until she reached the Mazda. Then she slid into the car and closed the door.

I'll wait for daylight, she told herself.

Exactly what she would do then, she wasn't sure.

When the car door opened two hours later, Alicia nearly screamed. She had been dozing, dreaming about being lost in a dark woods.

"Tr-Tracy?" Alicia could hardly get the word out.

Tracy slid behind the wheel. Slowly, she turned her head.

"Alicia. Hi." She spoke the words softly.

"Are you . . . all right?" Alicia asked. Tracy had the look of someone who had just awakened from a long sleep.

"I think so. I mean, I feel okay. A little out of focus, maybe." She smiled a half smile. "What happened?"

"You mean you don't remember?"

She wrinkled her brow. "I remember going to sleep . . . and I . . ." Her voice faded. She yawned.

"And what?" Alicia pressed.

"And that's all, I guess."

Alicia stared at her. "You don't remember driving here?"

Tracy shook her head.

"You don't remember the . . . the light?"

Tracy gave her a puzzled look. "What light?"

Alicia didn't know what to say.

They sat for a moment in silence. Tracy yawned again. Then she started the engine.

"What are you doing?" Alicia asked at once.

"Going home."

"Tracy, don't you . . . I mean, what was . . ." Alicia stopped.

"Can we talk in the morning?" Tracy said. "I really need to sleep. I'm beat."

Alicia looked at her in disbelief.

"That's it? Just, 'can we talk in the morning?' Don't you even want to know what we're doing here in the middle of the night?"

"What *are* we doing here?" Tracy asked.

Alicia had no answer. Maybe Tracy was right. Maybe the best thing to do was to talk in the morning.

"Tracy . . . aren't you . . . upset?"

Tracy yawned once more. She rubbed her eyes.

"Mainly what I am is . . . tired. And confused."

Not as confused as I am, Alicia thought.

Chapter 10

"Will you come with me?" Alicia asked.

"Oh, please," Debra said. "You're not really going to wander around Jackson Field in the rain."

"It's not raining anymore."

"It's a waste of time."

"I want to look around."

Debra rolled her eyes. "Look around for what?"

They were sitting in Debra's car after school on Wednesday. Alicia had told Debra about the night before. Debra had looked at her as though she'd lost her mind.

"I'm not sure."

"Oh, good. That helps."

"Do you believe a word of what I told you?"

Debra smiled. "You have to admit that your story's more than a little off the wall."

"Do you or don't you?"

Alicia was dead serious. This troubled Debra. In all the years they'd been friends, Alicia had always been a solid, down-to-earth kid. As far as Debra knew, Alicia didn't drink or do drugs. But this talk about zombies and bright lights made her wonder.

"Did you tell Ryan?" Debra asked.

"No. Just you."

"How come?"

"Ryan will think I'm crazy."

"And I won't?"

"You've known me a lot longer, Deb."

They held each other's gaze for a moment. She looks tired, Debra thought.

"So," Alicia said, "do you or don't you?"

Debra sighed. "All right, all right. I'll come with you."

"You didn't answer my question."

Debra turned serious. "Look, Alicia, I'm trying. I believe something happened last night. What it was exactly and why . . . well . . ." She didn't finish the sentence. "Truthfully, if I were hearing this stuff from anyone but you, I'd already be long gone."

"Thank you. I think."

Debra started the engine. She glanced at her friend.

"You and Tracy weren't smoking anything, were you?"

"Drive the car, Deb."

"Just asking."

She put the car in gear and headed toward the field.

"Tell me again what Tracy said when you spoke with her this morning," Debra said.

Alicia ran a hand through her hair. "She didn't say much of anything. She was quiet."

"How'd she act?"

"Same as always. Just more low key." Alicia shook her head. "It's weird. I would've been freaked. She acted like nothing much happened."

"Like you said, she doesn't remember anything. So, as far as she knows, nothing did happen."

"Except that we were sitting in her car in front of Jackson Field in the middle of the night," Alicia said. "And it sure wasn't *me* who drove us there."

Debra smiled. "Now, *that* I can believe."

"You're a hateful person, you know that?"

Debra laughed.

They parked near the entrance. It was a gray, cloudy day. Except for three teens throwing a ball around, Jackson Field was empty.

Alicia paused as she walked onto the field.

"It looks so different in daylight."

Debra didn't answer. She had no clue what went on last night. And she didn't know why they were here now. But if Alicia needed her, she'd be there. Alicia would do the same for her. Of course, Debra couldn't imagine ever taking Alicia on a wild-goose chase like this.

Alicia started walking. Debra hesitated, then followed.

"You know," Debra said, "if you tell me what I'm looking for, I can be more help."

"I don't know," Alicia said. "Anything unusual."

"Anything unusual," Debra repeated. "Right." She shook her head. *I think the girl's losing it.*

They strolled across the field. Alicia searched the ground, alert for any clue to last night's events. She tried to follow the same path she had taken with Tracy. But judging the direction and distance was impossible.

After ten minutes, she stopped. She looked at Debra.

"This is stupid. All I see is grass, rocks, and dirt."

"I saw a squirrel," Debra said.

"Very funny."

"Oh, lighten up, Alicia. I'm sure there's a simple explanation for whatever happened."

"Such as?"

Debra tried, but she couldn't come up with one.

"We may as well go," Alicia said.

"No argument from me."

They turned and walked back toward the car.

Behind them, thirty yards away, a brown rock softly vibrated.

Chapter 11

By Friday afternoon, Alicia was starting to doubt her sanity.

Things seemed wrong to her. There was no other way to put it. But how much was real? And how much was she imagining?

It wasn't just that night at Jackson Field, although that was by far the strangest thing of all. It was other things. Little things. Things that seemed . . . odd. At least, they seemed odd to Alicia.

Like Nick Santiago. Alicia hadn't heard Nick tell a joke all week. Not a big deal with any other kid. But Nick always told jokes. When she talked with him, he seemed the same as ever. Not depressed. Not sad. Not upset about anything. Just fine. But no jokes.

Then there was Gina and Matt. The word was they might be breaking up. That was like Romeo and Juliet splitting. Ryan had asked Matt about it. Matt said Gina was hassling him. But Alicia had never heard Gina get on Matt for anything.

And Rachel. At the party, Rachel had been troubled by her "sleepwalking" experience. But when Alicia had raised the subject again yesterday, Rachel had tried to blow the whole thing off. Said she felt embarrassed.

And Tracy. Now, that really bothered Alicia. Tracy acted as if that night at the Field had all been a bad dream. Whenever Alicia brought it up, Tracy said little. Alicia expected some reaction from her. Curiosity. Worry. Horror. Something. But Tracy just frowned and shook her head. Like she was trying to deny that anything unusual had even happened.

Otherwise, she was the same old Tracy. The same, from her irritating comments to her fancy clothes. The same, except for one thing. Tracy Mason—straight-A Tracy—had gotten a C on a history test and a D on a science quiz. About those grades, Tracy *was* upset. But she had no explanation.

The flu bug going around might explain some of what felt "wrong" to Alicia. Some, but not all. And certainly not Tracy's disappearing act in Jackson Field.

Chapter 12

Debra pulled into Alicia's driveway. Alicia gathered her packages. It was Saturday afternoon. They'd been shopping at the mall in Chesterdale. Chesterdale was about five miles west of Monroe.

"What time's Ryan coming?" Debra asked.

"Seven. I'm cooking dinner."

Debra grinned. "There goes the relationship."

"Big words coming from someone who burns spaghetti."

"Hey, Reggie ate it, didn't he?"

"Reggie would eat anything," Alicia said with a laugh. "Mice, if you cooked them."

"Got a recipe?"

"Go home." Alicia got out of the car. "Thanks for driving."

"Next time it's your turn."

"Don't start." Alicia headed up the path to her front door.

"Hey, Alicia."

She stopped. "What?"

"Is he staying over?"

Alicia gave her a look. "I'll tell you tomorrow."

Debra winked. "Don't do anything I wouldn't do."

"There *is* nothing you wouldn't do."

Alicia hummed as she washed greens for the salad. She felt more relaxed than she had all week. Shopping with Debra was always a blast. It took her mind off school and Tracy and Jackson Field.

Mrs. Lyons called from Florida. She needed to stay with Grandma at least a few more days. Alicia told her no problem. Everything was under control. Her mother asked how things went at Tracy's house. Alicia said fine. She wanted to focus only on Ryan tonight. She didn't even want to think about that evening with Tracy.

At five past seven, Alicia heard Ryan's car in the driveway. The doorbell rang a moment later. As soon as she opened the door, Alicia sensed something wasn't right. She saw it in Ryan's face. Nothing obvious. But when you spend enough time with someone, you just know.

"Hi." He came in and kissed her hello. "Something smells good."

"Chicken parmigiana."

"My favorite."

"Really?" Alicia smiled. "What a coincidence."

He smiled back. "I'll bet."

They walked to the kitchen together. Ryan helped put the finishing touches on the salad. They chatted easily. But Ryan was quieter than usual.

"You okay?" Alicia asked, once they'd sat down to eat.

"Sure. Why?"

"You seem a little . . . subdued."

"No, I'm fine." He took a big bite of chicken. "Hey, this is great," he said changing the subject.

"Thanks."

Alicia watched him a moment. She remembered when he'd twisted his ankle in a soccer game. Afterwards, he could hardly walk. But he wouldn't talk about it. "I'm fine," he kept saying. He'd had the same look on his face then. *The mask of male pride,* Debra liked to call it.

It wasn't until dessert that Ryan finally asked for some aspirin. Alicia wasn't surprised. She'd already guessed. All through dinner, she'd hoped it was something else. But a part of her had known what was coming.

She brought him the aspirin. "Headaches seem to be the in thing lately," she said. She tried to sound more cheerful than she felt.

"Yeah, I know. Jay had a killer last week." Jay Enslow was one of Ryan's close friends. "Maybe I caught the bug from him."

"Maybe," Alicia said. There was a knot in her stomach. "When did it start?"

"This afternoon." He swallowed the aspirin. "Wasn't so bad at first. Been getting worse."

"You could have called me, you know. I would have understood."

He smiled. "What? And missed your chicken parmigiana?"

"And my empty house . . ."

"Never entered my mind."

"I'm sure."

They did the dishes. Then they went into the living room. Alicia popped a tape into the VCR. A recent Mel Gibson movie. They sat down on the couch. Alicia tried not to think about Rachel's story. And she tried even harder not to think about Tracy. But she couldn't concentrate on the movie. She was worried.

Ryan's headache was getting worse. He tried to hide it. But she could see it in his pained expression.

By 10:00, even Ryan was no longer trying to pretend. His head was throbbing.

"Feels like an army marching through my head," he said. "In combat boots." He rubbed his eyes." I think I should go."

"No."

Alicia spoke the word so sharply, they were both surprised. Ryan gave her a questioning look.

"Don't go," Alicia insisted. "Stay over." All of a sudden, she was really scared. Not for herself. For Ryan.

"Music to my ears," he said, forcing a smile. "Only thing is, I'm in no shape to—"

"I mean, just stay over. If you're sick, I'll take care of you." Alicia hoped that he didn't take this the wrong way. Ryan didn't like being fussed over.

He gave her a long look. "I won't be good company. Not feeling like this."

"That's okay."

"I don't think—"

"Please, Ry."

Alicia saw the puzzled look on his face. For an instant, she almost told him about Tracy. But then she decided that now was not the time. If ever.

"I'm just worried about you," she explained. "Anyway, if you feel better tomorrow, we can have breakfast together." She tried to sound lighthearted. "It'll be fun."

Ryan couldn't help but smile. "Thanks." He kissed her. "How can I refuse an offer like that?"

He called his parents. He said he was staying over at Jay Enslow's house. Then he called Jay. No one was home. He left a message on Jay's answering machine. Ryan sometimes covered for Jay, too. What were friends for?

They turned off the movie before it was over. Neither of them was really paying attention.

"Want to call it a night?" Alicia asked.

"Yeah. I guess. I'm really beat. And my head feels like a bass drum. What a bummer."

"Come on." She stood and held out her hand. "I'm putting you to bed." They went upstairs together.

"You want the guest room or my room?" Alicia asked.

This was a private joke. They had shared Alicia's bed before. But she had threatened to make Ryan sleep in the guest room if he couldn't take no for an answer.

"I don't think there'll be a problem tonight," Ryan said. "For which I'm sorry," he added.

She kissed his cheek. "Me too."

They started for Alicia's room. Ryan hesitated.

"You know, maybe we shouldn't be together. I wouldn't want you to catch whatever I have."

Alicia smiled. "It's a little late to worry about that. Besides, this headache thing is going around school." *And I want you where I can see you,* she thought.

Ryan stripped to his shorts. Then he slipped under the top sheet. "Sorry about tonight," he said. "Dinner was terrific."

"Thanks."

His eyes slowly closed.

"I'm so tired . . ."

"You want some water or something?" Alicia asked.

He yawned. "No . . . that's okay."

"Should I leave some aspirin for you on the night table?"

No answer.

"Ry?"

He was asleep.

Alicia looked at the clock. Just past 11:00. She thought back to that evening with Tracy. They had gone to bed about the same time. Tracy, too, had complained of a headache. And then she had awakened about 1:30. Well, not exactly awakened . . .

Alicia felt a chill along her spine. She remembered the nightmare car ride to Jackson Field.

Stop it, she told herself.

She sat down on the edge of the bed. She watched Ryan. His breathing was slow and easy.

Could just be a headache, she thought. People do get simple, ordinary headaches. Doesn't mean they're all going to turn into zombies.

You're being stupid, she told herself. *You're letting your imagination run wild.*

Chapter 13

At midnight Alicia called Debra from the downstairs phone. Ryan was sleeping soundly. In fact, he'd hardly moved. But Alicia was still spooked. She was afraid to go to sleep. She kept thinking about Tracy.

Debra's answering machine picked up. Alicia wasn't surprised. Debra and Reggie had gone to a party in Chesterdale. Debra's nutty cousin Valerie lived there. Valerie's parties always ran late.

"So where are you when I need you?" Alicia said into the phone machine. "Ryan's here, but he's out for the count. Listen, Deb . . . I was . . ." She hesitated. *I hate talking to machines.* "I was just calling . . . well, you know . . . that whole business with Tracy . . ." She stopped. *Where am I going with this?* "Oh, never mind. I'm being ridiculous. I'm going to bed. Talk to you tomorrow. Bye."

She hung up. Now she felt foolish for having called.

She went back up to her room. Ryan was sleeping peacefully. Alicia smiled at his good looks. She imagined what the evening could have been like. *What a shame,* she thought.

She brushed her teeth and got ready for bed. Then she slipped in beside him. Gently, she kissed his cheek.

"Night," she whispered. Ryan didn't stir.

Alicia turned off the lamp.

Ten minutes later she was up again. She went to her closet and found a flashlight. It was an old one. She had written *Alicia* on the black handle in pink nail polish. She found two fresh batteries for it. Then she put the flashlight on the night table and got back into bed.

Just in case, she told herself.

She closed her eyes.

She was still awake at 12:45 A.M.

And at 1:00.

And at 1:15.

Every time she'd start to drift off, Ryan would move an arm or a leg and Alicia would wake up.

Ryan is fine. I, on the other hand, am losing my mind.

She went down to the kitchen for a glass of juice. The house was silent. She wondered how Grandma was doing.

She went back upstairs. Ryan was sleeping quietly.

That's it, Alicia told herself. *Enough is enough.*

She got into bed and switched off the light. She focused her thoughts on pleasant memories. Summer days. Favorite movies. Ryan.

She moved closer to Ryan, so that their legs were touching. His warmth made her smile. She liked lying beside him.

A few minutes later, Alicia was asleep.

At 2:05 A.M., Ryan sat up in bed. His eyes were wide open.

Chapter 14

When it finally happened, Alicia felt almost relieved. In a way, the fear had been worse than the reality.

The instant Ryan sat up, Alicia was awake. She watched him. Her heart was pounding.

His movements were just like Tracy's. Steady. Unrushed. His eyes were open but looking straight ahead.

"Ryan?" she whispered. "Can you hear me?"

He was out of bed now, getting dressed. Just as Tracy had done.

Alicia didn't waste any time. She began putting on her own clothes.

She called his name twice more. He didn't answer. Alicia knew he wouldn't.

He put on his shoes and headed for the door. Alicia grabbed her flashlight and followed. Her stomach was an iron knot.

Stay cool, she told herself. *Tracy was fine. Ryan will be fine too.*

She prayed that she was right.

Ryan started down the stairs. Alicia was right behind him.

She knew where he was headed. She was sure of it.

And this time I'm going to find out what the hell is going on.

She wished there was time to call Debra. But Ryan was already opening the front door. She had to keep up.

He walked down the path toward the blue Ford in the driveway. Alicia ran around to the passenger side.

Deja vu, she thought, getting in.

Ryan slid behind the wheel. He started the engine.

Alicia was surprised that she felt as calm as she did. *I must be numb*, she thought. *Or crazy*.

She watched Ryan back the car out and start up the street. He drove with complete control. Just as Tracy had. And like hers, his face was a blank.

Ryan took Browning Drive into Harrow Street. Two cars passed them. Saturday night traffic in Monroe.

He turned onto Old Hills Road. Alicia knew he would.

They passed the high school, then turned onto Glen Lane.

Alicia's mouth was dry as sand. She remembered the dark field. The sudden light. And she was scared.

"Ryan?"

No answer.

He pulled up near the entrance. Beyond the streetlight, Jackson Field was an ocean of darkness.

Ryan shut off the motor. He opened the door and stepped out.

For an instant, Alicia couldn't move. Her legs were stone.

"Ryan," she whispered. She watched him through the windshield. The darkness seemed to swallow him as he moved toward the field.

Alicia suddenly felt very cold.

I wish Deb were here.

She got out of the car. She gripped the flashlight tightly. Like a weapon.

She started walking.

Chapter 15

Ryan walked faster than Tracy had. Alicia had to hurry if she hoped to catch up. The bigger flashlight helped. But she still had to take care to keep from tripping on the uneven ground.

Crossing the black field felt even creepier than it had the first time. Like reliving a nightmare, Alicia thought. Except this time it was Ryan in the nightmare with her.

And this time she had to be ready.

Alicia had no idea what happened to Tracy that night. But one thing was sure. She wasn't letting Ryan out of her sight. Tracy had gotten too far ahead of her. Alicia wasn't going to make the same mistake twice.

Something squealed in the darkness. Alicia nearly jumped out of her sneakers.

Raccoon? Cat, maybe?

Forget it, she told herself. *Catch up with Ryan.*

Alicia's hand tightened around the flashlight. Ryan was less than ten paces ahead now.

How far had Tracy walked before that flash of light? Alicia tried to move faster. It was so hard to judge distance in the dark. She had to get closer to Ryan. She didn't want to take any chances.

Her heart was hammering. Ryan was still about eight steps ahead of her.

She remembered how shocking that sudden light had been. Like a silent explosion. She tried to brace herself.

Ryan was just six paces ahead now. Just another minute, and she'd be right—

The blast of light stopped Alicia like a wall. She staggered back, dropping the flashlight. She shielded her eyes. For an instant, she couldn't see anything.

"Ryan!" she cried out.

Ryan kept walking.

The light was even more intense than Alicia had remembered. It was like the noon sun in a night sky.

Blindly, Alicia lurched forward.

"Ry!"

She squinted into the light. It was just like last time: a large rectangle shape. Like a doorway of light. The light seemed to come from the ground, as though from a projector beam.

But that was impossible. There was nothing on the ground but dirt and weeds and rocks.

Ryan moved ahead. He was going right into the light.

Alicia threw herself forward. She fell and got up again.

I have to stay with him. Have to.

Ryan was only a few steps ahead. He was almost within her reach.

And then, in one awful instant, he was gone.

"No!"

Alicia froze. The doorway of light was three feet in front of her. She could almost touch it.

Her mind raced. Last time, the light went out seconds after Tracy vanished. If Alicia stopped now, she would have gained nothing. She knew no more than she had before.

And Ryan . . . what about Ryan?

Go after him, her mind screamed. *Go* now. *Go after Ryan.*

But she was terrified. Her legs wouldn't move. Her heart was pounding.

Go now. There's no more time.

She stared into the light. It hurt her eyes.

Go!

Alicia clenched her teeth. Then she flung herself into the light.

Chapter 16

The feeling was so strange. Like nothing Alicia had ever experienced.

She had lost all her bearings. There was no up, no down. No forward or backward. Just glaring light all around her.

Flying through water. It was a little like that. Plunging into a swimming pool from the high diving board. Alicia had a sense of speed, of motion. Yet, she didn't actually seem to be moving. And there was no water.

Every inch of her body tingled. She heard a faint whistling sound.

What's happening to me?

She squeezed her eyes shut against the light. It was so brilliant that it was painful. Alicia feared the light would burn through her eyelids.

Burn.

The word stuck in Alicia's mind. Powerful as the light was, it was not hot. In fact, she felt cool.

Time had stopped. She was trapped in a tunnel of light. She couldn't feel her arms or legs.

Her brain ran at half speed. She found it hard to finish a thought.

Am I dying? she wondered. *Am I already dead?*

Blue. Pale blue.

Alicia blinked her eyes. She was in a room of some sort. The room was bathed in blue light. She was standing.

She felt dizzy. Like she'd just come off a killer roller coaster. She put a hand out to brace herself against a wall. The wall was cold.

Metal?

She frowned.

Metal walls?

She tried to focus her thoughts. She didn't remember coming into this room. Yet, here she was. Standing here.

Standing where?

Where am I?

Slowly, her mind began to clear. She remembered Jackson Field. The bright light. Ryan.

Where was Ryan?

She took a closer look around. The room was very small. Square. And empty. No chairs or tables. No lamps. Nothing. She couldn't tell where the blue light was coming from.

The room had no windows. But a panel on one bare wall looked like it might be a door.

A chill ran through Alicia. *What is this place?*

She looked up at the ceiling. Tiny patterns. Made of what? Wires? Printed circuits? Computer chips? No way to tell. They were so small.

She listened for some sound. She heard nothing.

Alicia suddenly felt more alone than she ever had in her life.

She moved to the panel. There was no handle or knob. No button. But in the center of the panel, there was a circle. Within the circle, she saw a symbol. She didn't recognize it.

She reached out her fingers. They were trembling.

She touched the circle. Instantly the panel slid open.

Alicia jumped back, startled. She'd never seen such a door.

Through the doorway, she saw a corridor. She peeked outside. The corridor was well lit. She looked in one direction, then the other.

The corridor curved both left and right. It was empty. Alicia heard a soft hum. An air conditioner, maybe. Or a motor. Hard to tell. She heard other sounds, too. But they were too far away to recognize.

Alicia stepped into the corridor. It was cool. Almost cold. She glanced around. On the wall beside the doorway were more circles. They all contained symbols. None looked familiar.

Alicia chewed her lip. She didn't like this. Didn't like any of this.

Go left or right? she wondered. It didn't matter.

She started walking to the left. She moved slowly. Her sneakers made no sound. The floor was well padded.

She came to an open doorway. Next to the doorway were more circles, more odd symbols.

Carefully, Alicia looked into the room. It was exactly like the room she'd just left.

She kept walking.

She passed more rooms. All empty. All the same.

Distant sounds. Still too far away to identify.

She continued walking.

She rounded a corner and came to a larger room. She stared through the open door. She saw what looked like chairs and tables. But they were different from any that Alicia had ever seen. The chairs were bigger, wider. They were shiny black. They rested on only one thick leg. The tables were shiny black, too. They had no legs at all. They seemed to just hang in the air.

Fear gripped her. Her throat was so dry, it hurt to swallow.

Where am I?

She wished she were home. She wished she were with Ryan or Deb. She wished she were anywhere but here.

Wherever "here" was.

She continued down the corridor. Were the sounds getting louder? She wasn't sure. For a moment, she thought she heard far-off voices. Then they stopped.

More rooms. Different sizes now. Some large, some small. Most were only dimly lit. No windows. Alicia could make out more shiny black tables and chairs. She saw other objects, too. Things she'd never seen before. Some looked like machines. A few had tiny glowing dials. Others resembled small TV sets.

In some rooms, tables were covered with smaller objects. Tools of various sizes and shapes. Something that looked like a wristwatch. Colored jars and bottles. A device that resembled a microscope. And many other items that Alicia couldn't even begin to identify.

Alicia racked her brain. There had to be some explanation. Could this be a museum? Some kind of school? A place for research, maybe? A factory? Nothing fit. There were too many unknown—

Alicia stopped. She'd heard voices again. At least, she thought they were voices. They sounded closer this time.

She followed the corridor until it ended in a T. She looked left and right. More rooms in both directions. She listened for the voices. They seemed to be coming from the right. She started toward them.

Along this new corridor, she found more closed doors. The rooms that were open looked like the other rooms Alicia had passed.

Whatever this place was, it was large. Alicia wondered if there were other floors. Had to be.

The corridor curved sharply left. Was that the buzz of voices she was hearing? She tried to make out words. Couldn't.

She kept walking. She glanced into several rooms. Empty.

Whoever used all these rooms was somewhere else in the building. Maybe they were all asleep. Not surprising. It was, after all, the middle of the nigh—

A clicking sound. Another. Then a hiss.

Alicia froze.

More clicks and hisses. Close by. They didn't sound like mechanical noises. They were the kinds of sounds people sometimes made. Like at the zoo, when people try to get the attention of animals.

Alicia slowly moved forward. She stayed close to the wall. The sounds seemed to be coming from a room just ahead.

Many clicks and hisses. Then silence. Then more clicks and hisses.

Alicia walked silently to the edge of the doorway. She kept her shoulder to the wall. Her heart was pounding.

Slowly, she leaned around and peeked into the room.

She gasped.

Oh my God—

Chapter 17

Alicia's mind couldn't grasp what she was seeing.

Couldn't grasp it and couldn't believe it.

She just stared. Petrified. Her fingers clutched the wall.

Inside the room was a large, circular black table. Around the table stood five . . . creatures.

They were not human.

They were about five feet tall. They had broad, heavy bodies and two thick legs. The bodies were covered with short gray hair. The hair was so dense, it looked like fur.

Each creature had four arms. But Alicia hardly paid attention to the arms. It was the head that jolted her.

Each creature had a large, squarish head. It, too, was covered with dense, gray hair. The front of the head—the face—had one big eye. There was a second big eye at the back of the head. Below the front eye, in place of a nose, were six or seven small openings. Underneath them was a wide mouth.

The creatures seemed to be working together. Their heads were bent over the table. As they worked, they made clicking and hissing sounds. Occasionally, one would speak what seemed like words. Then another would answer. Their voices sounded hoarse and whispery. The words were like none Alicia had ever heard.

The creatures had not seen Alicia. They were too busy with their project. They might never even have known she was there, if Alicia hadn't made a sound.

She didn't mean to. The sound bubbled up from inside her. It was just a soft cry of shock. Of fear.

But the gasp was enough.

The creature nearest the doorway lifted its head. Its rear eye looked straight at Alicia. The eye was dark green.

Alicia drew back, terrified.

RUN! her mind screamed.

But there was nowhere to run to, and Alicia knew it.

The creature turned toward her. It made several sounds. The other creatures all looked up.

More hisses and clicks. Alicia wondered if the sounds had meaning. Maybe they were just body noises, like breathing. Or sounds like dolphins make.

The creatures moved around from behind the table. One or two of them spoke. The others kept silent.

Alicia stepped back from the doorway. Her legs felt rubbery. Her heart was racing.

Slowly, they came toward her. They were all staring at her. The one with the green eye was in front.

Alicia took another step back. And another. She was in the middle of the corridor now.

The creatures came closer. They looked much alike. But Alicia could see differences. Some were taller or heavier than others. Two had darker hair. One had a yellow eye. Two had red eyes. The smallest creature had a clear, colorless eye.

Alicia backed up two more steps. She was breathing in small gasps. The creatures kept coming. She heard their clicks and hisses.

They moved out of the room into the corridor. Alicia took two more backward steps. Then she felt the opposite wall against her back.

No place left to go.

Her entire body felt like ice. Her mind was a blank of terror.

The creatures gathered around her. Alicia stared into their big eyes, their alien faces.

"Please—" She tried to speak. But she couldn't get the words out.

The creature with the green eye reached one hand toward her. It had six hairy fingers.

"No—" Alicia shrank back in horror. "Please..."

The creature lowered its hand.

"Bloo . . . plaa . . . nett." The creature's words were a gruff whisper.

Alicia looked into the big green eye. It was studying her.

"Bloo . . . plaa . . . nett," the creature repeated slowly.

"Err-thh," the one with the yellow eye said.

Alicia pressed her back to the wall. She stared at them.

This can't be . . . just can't be . . .

Green Eye tried once more. "Bloo-plaa-nett." Two of its arms waved in the air. Some kind of gesture.

"Err-thh," Yellow Eye said again. The creature hissed and clicked.

They're . . . talking to me, Alicia thought. She couldn't believe it. Didn't *want to* believe it.

Who are they? What are they?

Green Eye moved closer. This time, the creature spoke more loudly, arms waving.

"Bloo-plaa-nett!"

It's getting frustrated, Alicia realized. Like someone trying to communicate with a foreigner. It wants to be understood.

"Yes . . ." she managed to reply. "Blue . . . planet." The words came out in a whisper. Her throat was desert dry.

Green Eye seemed to relax. It was pleased.

"Err-thh," Yellow Eye repeated.

"Earth," Alicia echoed.

Green Eye and Yellow Eye looked at each other. One of the creatures with dark hair said something in its strange language. Green Eye answered. Yellow Eye seemed to disagree. Then the smallest creature, the one with the colorless eye, suddenly reached out and touched Alicia.

She screamed. The touch hadn't hurt. But it had startled her.

All the creatures jumped back. They hissed and clicked. Their arms waved.

Yellow Eye spoke sharply to Alicia. She couldn't understand the words. But the creature was clearly not pleased.

Green Eye said something to the creature who had touched her. Two of the other creatures began to speak. Then Yellow Eye interrupted. Before long, all five of them were talking at once.

They're arguing, Alicia thought, as the creatures raised their voices. Yellow Eye and Green Eye were the loudest. But all the creatures joined in the dispute.

Alicia clung to the wall. The harsh, angry sound of their voices frightened her.

The argument grew louder and louder. Arms waved wildly in the air. Hands pointed at her. There were grunts and hisses and clicks. Alicia shut her eyes against the awful scene.

And then, suddenly, the noise died down.

And stopped.

Alicia opened her eyes. She saw another creature approaching. This one was different from the others. It was bigger. Much bigger.

It was nearly seven feet tall, Alicia guessed. Its arms and legs looked stronger, more powerful than those of the other creatures. The gray hair covering its body was white at the tips.

Alicia's fear left her numb. She didn't move. Couldn't.

The huge creature stopped in front of her. Its large, dark eye stared down at her pale face. All the other creatures kept silent. After a moment, it turned and spoke to Green Eye. Its voice was low and rough like the others' voices. But it was deeper, stronger.

Green Eye responded at once. Then Yellow Eye spoke. The big creature listened. Then it turned back to Alicia.

"I am Dal," it said. It spoke slowly. The words were hard to understand. But they were in English. "How came you here?"

Alicia peered up at the huge creature. She didn't know what to say.

"How came you here?" it repeated more loudly. One of its long arms impatiently slapped at the air.

Alicia winced. "I . . . I don't know."

Dal clicked and hissed. Then it spoke again to Green Eye. Yellow Eye cut in. The two smaller creatures began to argue once more.

Without warning, two of Dal's arms shot out. They struck both creatures across the face. Dal snapped several words at them. The words were fierce and furious. The two creatures instantly fell silent. The others drew back. They were clearly afraid of Dal.

This must be the adult, Alicia suddenly realized. *The others are . . . what? Kids?* It was hard to imagine.

Dal looked again at Alicia. She could almost feel the dark, cold eye pierce her. Abruptly, the creature turned. It growled a command to Green Eye. Then it walked away. Its rear eye continued to watch.

Two of Green Eye's hands grabbed Alicia's arm. They pulled her down the corridor in the direction Dal had gone.

Chapter 18

Debra didn't get home from her cousin Valerie's party till after 2:00 A.M. She was beat.

She walked up the stairs quietly. Her parents and younger sisters were asleep. Debra was glad. Her mother always gave her a hard time for coming home late. Her father, though, probably wouldn't have said much. After all, nutty Valerie was from his side of the family. And anyway, her father liked Reggie and trusted him to bring his daughter home safe.

Debra saw the blinking red light as soon as she walked into her bedroom. She kicked off her shoes and plopped down on the bed. She hit the answering machine button. When she heard Alicia's voice, she smiled.

"So where are you when I need you? Ryan's here, but he's out for the count. Listen, Deb . . . I was . . . I was just calling . . . well, you know . . . that whole business with Tracy . . . Oh, never mind. I'm being ridiculous. I'm going to bed. Talk to you tomorrow. Bye."

Debra chuckled and shook her head. "Glad to hear you're getting it together," she said to the machine. She had all but forgotten Alicia's crazy story about Tracy and Jackson Field. Besides, Debra was more interested in why Ryan was "out for the count." She wondered what Alicia had done to tire him out.

"You have a dirty mind," she said to herself. She went to the bathroom to brush her teeth.

Chapter 19

Green Eye's grip on Alicia's arm was firm but not painful. She felt the strength in the creature's fingers. If this was a "kid," she could only imagine how powerful Dal must be. She wondered if Green Eye was male or female — if these creatures *had* males and females. For all Alicia knew, they could all be one sex. Or four different sexes. Anything was possible.

Dal led the way down the corridor. Green Eye and Alicia were several steps behind. They had to walk fast to keep up with Dal's long legs. Yellow Eye and the others followed.

Dal stopped beside a wide metal door. The creature barked another command at Green Eye. Then it walked off. Green Eye did not follow.

Yellow Eye and the others caught up. Yellow Eye looked at Green Eye. The two spoke briefly. The others waited in silence.

Alicia sensed a shift in the creatures' mood. Before, they had been excited. Curious, maybe.

Dal had changed that. Now all the creatures seemed glum.

Like kids who have been scolded, Alicia thought. She wondered if Dal was their parent.

Green Eye and Yellow Eye ended their talk. Green Eye said something to the other three creatures. They hesitated. But after a moment, they slowly walked away. No one spoke to Alicia.

Green Eye touched a circle on the wall beside the door. The door slid open. Green Eye pulled Alicia inside. Yellow Eye followed.

The room looked much like the one Alicia had arrived in. But it was slightly larger.

There was a control panel beside the door. Green Eye touched a symbol. The door closed. An instant later, there was a flash of light.

The door opened again. Alicia blinked in surprise. She was looking out at a different corridor.

It must be an elevator . . .

But how could it be? The "ride" between floors had taken only seconds. How many floors could they possibly have traveled? Two? Four? Twenty? She had no idea.

In fact, she wasn't even sure they had moved from one "floor" to another. For all she knew, this "elevator" had beamed them to another building. Or, to a whole other . . . place.

The idea chilled her. If a brief flash of light could move them here, how far had she traveled when she stepped through the light in Jackson Field?

"Where . . . are we?" Alicia asked. Her voice sounded shaky. She was fighting against panic.

Green Eye looked at her, but did not answer. He pulled her out into the corridor. Yellow Eye followed.

They began walking. There were fewer rooms along this corridor. But the rooms were larger. There were many symbols on the walls.

Neither Green Eye nor Yellow Eye spoke. The only sounds they made were occasional clicks and hisses. Green Eye kept one hand on Alicia's arm as they walked.

Alicia kept telling herself to stay calm. Crying or screaming would do her no good. She had to try and think.

How often had she heard stories about aliens kidnapping humans? Usually, she heard them on TV. Or saw them in silly supermarket newspapers. Headlines like, *I Was Captured by a UFO* or *Martians Took My Baby*.

She had never believed any of those tales. No one did. Aliens were no more real than movie monsters.

Until now.

"Please . . ." Alicia tried again. "Tell me where we are."

They both glanced at her in silence. They kept walking.

Maybe they don't understand the question, Alicia thought. Dal had seemed more comfortable speaking English words than these two creatures had. Maybe Dal was the teacher, and they were the students.

But how had any of them learned English?

And why?

A hundred questions buzzed around in Alicia's head. But no answers.

She tried using words they knew.

"Blue planet . . . Earth. Where?"

The two creatures looked at each other. They exchanged words in their own language.

Maybe they do understand the question, Alicia thought. Maybe they just don't know the words to answer. She was about to ask again, when Green Eye spoke.

"Far," the creature said. "Earth far away."

The corridor curved to the left. Yellow Eye said something Alicia did not understand. Green Eye grunted. Alicia sensed that the two creatures didn't get along. Maybe they were siblings. Or rivals. Or both.

They turned the corner. Ahead, some sort of gate blocked their path. They walked up to it and stopped.

The gate was formed of crisscrossed bars. They were thick metal, like those of a jail cell.

There was a row of circles on the wall. Below the circles were several lines of symbols. They were large and looked important.

Yellow Eye touched one of the circles. An overhead light started to blink. Yellow Eye touched another circle. The gate parted in the middle. The two sections slowly began to slide apart. They opened about 15 inches. Then they just stopped. The light ceased blinking.

The two creatures glanced at each other. Both appeared puzzled. Yellow Eye spoke a few words. Green Eye did not seem to agree.

Suddenly, Yellow Eye pounded one hand against each half of the gate. Nothing happened. Yellow Eye hit the metal bars again. Neither section of the gate moved. The creature made a low growling sound. Alicia had a feeling he was cursing. That is, if these creatures cursed.

Green Eye and Yellow Eye argued over what to do. Clearly, the gate was not working as it was supposed to.

Yellow Eye slapped two circles at once. Green Eye protested loudly. Alicia could hear the alarm in the creature's voice. *This is nothing to fool around with,* Green Eye seemed to be saying. Yellow Eye ignored the complaint and hit both circles again.

The overhead light blinked twice, then stopped. Both parts of the gate suddenly slammed shut with a loud clang. Then they opened about 12 inches—and slammed shut again.

Green Eye spoke sharply to the other creature. Yellow Eye paid no attention. Green Eye turned away, as if to leave. Alicia felt the creature pulling her arm.

Yellow Eye snapped several words at Green Eye. Two of Yellow Eye's arms cut the air in annoyance. Then Yellow Eye punched at the circles again.

The overhead light blinked. The two sections of the heavy gate began to slide apart again. Abruptly, they stopped. Then they opened a few more inches, and stopped again. The light kept blinking.

They waited. The gate was still only partway open. But now there was enough room for them to pass through one at a time.

Yellow Eye lifted its head in triumph. The creature started to walk forward. Green Eye tried to grab Yellow Eye.

Yellow Eye growled and knocked the hand away. Slowly, Yellow Eye squeezed between the two metal sections. It had to turn sideways to fit its broad body through the opening.

Yellow Eye faced Green Eye. It said a few words. It moved its head from side to side. Its hands fluttered in the air.

It's teasing him, Alicia realized. *Like one kid calling another kid "chicken."*

Alicia felt Green Eye's fingers tightening on her arm. The creature was getting angry.

Yellow Eye kept fluttering its hands. The overhead light was still blinking. Green Eye hesitated.

Yellow Eye called out something to the other creature. Alicia could almost guess what it was. Some things were clear in any language.

Green Eye suddenly pulled Alicia over to the opening in the gate. She was much thinner than either of the two creatures. Her body would fit through easily. Before she could protest, Green Eye pushed her forward. Alicia nearly fell, but Yellow Eye caught her arm and held her.

Green Eye came up to the opening. Its head moved nervously back and forth. Green Eye was bigger than Yellow Eye. It would be a tighter fit.

Yellow Eye waved an arm impatiently. Alicia felt the creature's fingers digging into her arm. Yellow Eye's grip was less gentle than Green Eye's.

Green Eye hissed and clicked. It inched closer to the opening, then stopped. It glared at Yellow Eye. Yellow Eye grunted. Finally, Green Eye turned its body to one side and started through the gate.

At that instant, the overhead light stopped blinking. The two parts of the gate snapped together like steel jaws.

Chapter 20

Green Eye squealed. Alicia had never heard such a horrible sound. The gate had slammed onto the creature's chest. Green Eye was trapped between the metal sections.

Yellow Eye jumped back in shock. All of its arms waved through the air.

Green Eye was gasping and snorting. It tried to push against the metal. But the heavy gate had the creature pinned.

"Do something!" Alicia cried to Yellow Eye.

Yellow Eye dropped its grip on Alicia's arm. It took a step forward, then stopped.

"Help him!" Alicia screamed. "It's crushing him!"

She looked at one wall, then the other. But there was no control panel on this side of the gate.

"Please!"

She tried to pull Yellow Eye forward. She hoped the creature was strong enough to move the gate. At least it could try.

But Yellow Eye wouldn't move. The creature was in a panic. It rocked frantically from side to side. It called out to Green Eye. Then, suddenly, it turned and bolted down the corridor.

Green Eye's gasps and squeals were awful. The creature's head was jerking from side to side. All four arms were banging against the gate.

Alicia grabbed the metal bars. She pulled with all her might. But she couldn't budge the gate.

"Help!" she shouted. "Help!" Her cries sounded hollow in the empty corridor.

Green Eye pawed at the bars. Its wide mouth was open, gasping. Its big eye was filled with pain and terror.

Alicia looked around for something to help. Some object, anything. But there was nothing.

The control panel on the other side of the gate was her only hope. She ran toward it. She reached through the bars. If the gate suddenly flew open, it would probably break her arm. But she couldn't worry about that now.

She stretched and strained. But her fingers couldn't reach the panel. She knew she wouldn't be able to. The gate was meant to be opened from one side only. Otherwise, there would be controls on both sides.

Green Eye's cries tore at Alicia's heart. In that moment, the creature was no longer a frightening, nonhuman being. It was someone in pain, a child maybe. Someone who would die if she couldn't help him.

Chapter 21

Ryan rubbed his eyes. He felt groggy . . . out of it. Like when he woke up after he'd had his appendix taken out.

He blinked several times and looked around.

"What the—?"

He was sitting in his car. The motor was running. The car was parked in Alicia's driveway.

Ryan tried to clear his head. He tried to remember how he'd gotten here. But all he could recall was having dinner with Alicia. Having dinner, then going to bed because of that stupid headache. Well, at least *that* was gone.

He checked his watch. Almost six in the morning. What was he doing out here in the driveway? And where was Alicia?

He turned off the engine and walked to the house. He tried the door. It was unlocked.

"Alicia?"

The house was silent.

He searched the first floor, then the second. There was no sign of her.

He sat down on the couch and tried to think. His head felt like it was filled with slush. And he was tired. So tired.

Had he been drinking? Was this a hangover?

But Alicia didn't drink. And Ryan didn't remember drinking anything. Neither of them did drugs.

He went to the bathroom and splashed cold water into his face. It didn't help.

He paced from the living room to the kitchen and back. He sat down on the couch again. He shook his head in frustration.

Dinner and bed. That's all he remembered.

What's going on?

And where's Alicia?

Chapter 22

Alicia shifted around on the soft mat. She tried to keep her eyes open. But she kept dozing. Scared as she was, she was also exhausted. She'd slept only half an hour before being awakened by Ryan.

The small room added to her sleepiness. It was warm and silent. The light was dim. There were no windows. The walls were bare. The room was almost empty. It contained only the floor mat, a table, and two chairs. A metal cylinder stood in one corner. Alicia guessed the cylinder was a toilet.

The two adult creatures had brought her to the room over an hour ago. Then they'd left without a word. The door had slid shut behind them. Unlike other doors Alicia had seen, this one had no controls. No circles or symbols.

The meaning was clear. The only control panel was on the outside. She was a prisoner.

Alicia wondered how much time had passed since Jackson Field. How long had she been here? Wherever *here* was. She wished she had her watch. But she'd left it on the night table when she'd chased after Ryan.

Alicia stared up at the blank ceiling. Her eyes felt so heavy. Her thoughts wandered. How strange it was not to know time and place. Time and place were reference points. Usually she took them for granted. Without them, she felt cut off. Like a boat . . . drifting . . .

She let her eyes close.

She was asleep.

It wasn't the door opening and closing that woke her. It was the hissing and clicking.

Alicia's eyes blinked open. She nearly screamed.

Green Eye was in the room. Beside Green Eye stood the green-eyed adult she had seen in the corridor.

Alicia scrambled to her feet. Like Dal, this adult was almost seven feet tall. She had to raise her head to meet the dark green eye.

"I am Leddu," the creature said. He glanced down at Green Eye. "This is Yonte. Yonte is—" The creature broke off. He looked at a small device in one of his hands. The device had a screen, like a calculator. Below the screen were many rows of symbols. Leddu spoke a word into the device in his own language. The word *son* appeared on the screen. "Yonte is my son."

Yonte walked toward Alicia. He moved stiffly. The gate had bruised him badly.

Alicia drew back. Yonte held out Alicia's sneaker and belt.

"These are yours." Yonte concentrated as he spoke. He wanted to get the English words right.

Alicia took the sneaker and belt. Her fingers trembled.

"Thank you." Her voice sounded almost as hoarse as Yonte's.

Yonte studied her a moment.

"Why . . ." He looked down at one hand. He was holding the same kind of device as his father. He spoke several words into it. English words appeared on the screen. "Why did you help me?"

Alicia glanced at Leddu. He was watching, listening.

"You were in pain." She spoke slowly, to help them understand her. "There was no one else."

Yonte let out a soft growl. "Braktor is a—" He had to check his word screen. "A coward. She did not help. She ran."

Alicia was surprised that Yellow Eye was female. She and Yonte looked and sounded much alike. Except for their eye color.

"I guess she went for help," Alicia said.

"Coward," Yonte snarled. "She is—"

Behind him, Leddu said something in their own language. Immediately, Yonte stopped speaking.

Alicia almost smiled. Leddu was like any parent. He didn't want his son calling other kids names.

Leddu moved closer. He eyed Alicia.

"Why did you help Yonte?" He hissed and clicked. "It is strong gate . . . could hurt you."

Alicia hesitated. Why was Leddu asking that same question again? Wasn't helping someone in pain reason enough?

"Yonte couldn't breathe," she answered. "He might have died."

Leddu tilted his head to one side. He seemed puzzled.

"But you are . . . ." He checked his word screen. "You are an alien."

This time Alicia did smile. She wondered if she looked as scary to them as they did to her.

"Wouldn't you have helped me?" she asked.

Leddu glanced at Yonte.

"You are an alien," he repeated.

Alicia did not like the way he said it. She sensed that Leddu looked down on her as a lesser being. A creature far inferior to himself.

In my eyes, you're the alien, Alicia wanted to say. But she feared Leddu would take this as an insult. She kept quiet.

"How came you here?" Leddu asked.

It was the same question Dal had asked earlier. Dal hadn't seemed pleased when she said she didn't know. This time, Alicia tried to explain. She explained how she had followed Ryan into the light.

Leddu listened closely. Alicia tried to judge his reaction. She couldn't. These creatures' faces did not show as much as human faces did. Not to her at least.

"You were not afraid?" Leddu asked when she was finished.

"Yes. I was afraid."

Yonte made a comment to his father in their own language.

Leddu kept his dark green eye on Alicia.

"Yonte says you are more brave than Braktor."

Brave or stupid, Alicia thought.

Leddu and Yonte spoke together. Yonte seemed to have more questions than his father had answers.

Alicia had a question of her own.

"Where is Ryan?" she asked when the two creatures had stopped talking.

"Ry-an?" Leddu repeated the word into his word screen. Apparently the device could also translate English words into their language. "I have no meaning for Ry-an."

Alicia kept her words simple. "Ryan was the boy who went through the light before me. But he wasn't in the room when I came."

Leddu thought for a moment. "There are many rooms. Many Ry-ans."

"But—"

Leddu cut her off. "I must go. I will talk with

you again."

Yonte asked his father a question. Leddu gave him a long look. Then he and his son spoke at length. Yonte seemed to be trying to convince Leddu of something. Alicia wished she could understand what they were saying. Finally, Leddu seemed to give in. He grunted. Then he fixed his big green eye on Alicia.

"Yonte will stay longer. You will answer his questions. Help him learn."

"Learn?" Alicia frowned. "Learn what?"

"About Earth people."

"I don't under—"

Leddu turned. His rear eye watched Alicia as he walked away. He pointed a small gray rod at the door. The door slid open.

Leddu paused at the doorway. He said several words into his word screen. Then he spoke to Alicia.

"I thank you." He hissed and clicked. "For helping Yonte."

He left the room. The door closed.

Chapter 23

Yonte wouldn't stop. Alicia felt drained. But Yonte was as sharp as ever.

They had been sitting at the table for hours. Alicia was on one side. Yonte sat across from her. At first, she had to strain to understand him. But slowly she got used to the hoarse whisper of his voice.

Yonte fired question after question at her. She had barely answered one when he asked another. Some were easy: *What is your school like?* Others were harder: *Why do so many Earth people harm one another?* Some were just funny: *Are you not cold with no hair on your body? How can you see behind you?*

The word screen helped Yonte ask his questions. But Alicia had to work to make her answers clear. Although Yonte had studied English, the language was still new to him.

Aside from the language problem, Yonte's abilities amazed Alicia. His mind was so fast—much faster than her own. Yonte grasped facts and concepts instantly. Equally amazing was his knowledge. No matter what subject, Yonte seemed to know more than Alicia. Much more.

It was scary. Yonte was young. If he were human, Alicia would guess him to be between 11 and 15. It was hard to judge. Sometimes he acted like a kid. Other times he seemed almost grown-up.

"Can we stop for a while?" Alicia asked.

"Why stop?"

"I'm tired."

Yonte considered this. "Why?"

Alicia smiled. Yonte had no idea how hard it was for her to keep up with him.

"Because you ask a billion questions."

Yonte spoke the word *billion* into his word screen.

"Not a billion," he said.

"I was exaggerating."

Yonte checked his word screen again. "Yes. Exaggerating."

"When will you answer *my* questions?" Alicia said. Several times she had tried to get information from him. Each time, he put her off.

"I will answer later."

"You said that before."

The two looked at each other. For a second, each forgot that the other was an alien being.

"I will answer later," Yonte repeated.

"That's not fair," Alicia said. She was surprised to hear the words come out of her mouth.

She was in no position to say what was fair and what wasn't.

Yonte said "fair" into his word screen. He tilted his head to one side. Alicia had learned that this motion meant he was puzzled.

"Fair? But you are an alien."

He said it the same way his father had said it.

"Meaning that I am not your equal?" Alicia asked. She tried to keep her voice calm. She didn't like being talked down to. Especially by a kid, human *or* alien.

Yonte fluttered a hand in the air. Alicia had seen the gesture before. Braktor had used it to tease Yonte at the gate.

"No," Yonte said. "How could you be?"

He didn't sound mean. He sounded surprised that she would even suggest such a thing.

Alicia didn't know what to say. In truth, she thought Yonte might be right. His people were far more advanced than humans. Still, she didn't like to be treated like some low form of animal life.

Before she could reply, the door slid open. It was Dal.

Yonte stood up at once. Alicia did the same.

Dal glanced at her. Then he spoke to Yonte. Yonte looked unhappy. He began to object. Dal's dark eye silenced him. Without another word, Dal walked out.

"It is time for my lessons," Yonte said. "I must go now."

Alicia felt her stomach knot. She didn't want to be left alone in the room again.

"But you haven't answered even one of my questions."

"I must go now," Yonte repeated. "We will talk more."

"At least tell me where we are. I don't even know that."

Yonte hesitated. "It is more easy for me to ask questions. I do not have all the words to answer."

"Please try, Yonte."

It was the first time she had called him by his name. It seemed to get his attention.

Yonte hissed and clicked. He spoke several words into his word screen. Then several more. He grunted.

"We are on a station," he began. "In space. Far from Earth."

Alicia's heart was pounding. She had already suspected that she was no longer on Earth. But she didn't want to believe it.

"How . . . far?"

Yonte used his word screen. "Millions of miles."

"But . . . that's impossible."

Yonte tilted his head. He just looked at her.

Alicia's legs felt suddenly weak. She had to sit down.

"This . . . station . . . ." Alicia's voice was little more than a whisper. "What . . . what is it for?"

"I do not understand."

"What is its . . . purpose?"

Yonte said "purpose" into his word screen. He thought a moment.

"Many purposes. Study. Learn. Explore. Experiment."

Alicia sensed that he was holding back.

"What—"

"Dal waits." Yonte moved toward the door. "I must go."

Alicia rose from the chair. "Yonte . . . ."

He paused.

Alicia struggled to ask the question most on her mind.

"Will you . . . ." She stopped, started again. Her heart raced. "When will you . . . let me go back?"

The question seemed to disturb him. "I cannot say. I am a learner. It is. . . ." He hesitated. Even with the word screen, it took some time for him to finish the thought. "It is a matter for the Three."

Alicia frowned. "The three what?"

"The Three: Dal, Nemm, and Leddu, my father. They are"—Yonte checked his screen—"in charge. They say what to do."

"Is Dal the leader?" Alicia asked, trying to understand.

"They are all the leader," Yonte said. "Together they speak as one."

Government by committee, Alicia thought. She was about to ask about Ryan. But Yonte was already in the corridor. He looked at Alicia through his rear eye. Then the door slid closed.

Chapter 24

Ryan dozed on Alicia's couch until 9:00 A.M. Then he splashed more cold water on his face and called Debra.

The phone rang three times. Debra rolled over in bed. She pulled the covers over her head. On the fourth ring, the answering machine picked up.

Ryan waited for the recorded message to end. He knew Debra had been out late.

"Debra? It's Ryan. Are you there?"

Debra buried her face in the pillow. "Go 'way," she mumbled.

"Deb? Pick up. It's important."

Debra's brain registered that it was Ryan calling her. This was unusual, especially on a Sunday morning. Her hand fumbled for the phone.

"Ummmm."

"Deb? It's Ryan. Is Alicia with you?"

"With *me?*" She opened her eyes. This question made no sense. "What are you talking about?"

Ryan hesitated. How in the world was he going to explain this?

"Ryan? You still there?" Debra was awake now. "What's up? You two have a fight?"

"No. Nothing like that. Listen . . . did you have breakfast yet?"

"Breakfast? You just woke me up. Do you think I ate breakfast and then went back to bed?" She sounded cranky.

"Okay, okay. I'm sorry. Can you meet me at the diner?"

"The diner? What's going on? Where's Alicia?"

"Half hour?"

"Ryan, what the—"

"I'll explain when I see you."

Ryan was waiting for Debra when she walked in. He waved to her from a booth in the corner.

"This better be good," Debra said, sitting down. "Not even Alicia calls me before 11:00 on a Sunday."

The waitress brought coffee. Debra ordered eggs. Ryan asked for an English muffin.

Ryan told her about the night before: having dinner with Alicia, going to sleep. Then waking up in her driveway.

Debra listened without interrupting. She did not like what she was hearing.

"You don't remember anything else?" she asked when he was finished.

Ryan shook his head. "Just what I told you."

"How's the headache now?"

"Gone. I'm fine. Just tired."

The waitress brought their orders. Debra wasn't hungry anymore.

"You sure Alicia didn't leave a note?" she asked.

"No note. I looked."

Debra fell silent, thinking.

Ryan leaned closer. "Do you remember the night of Peter's party?"

She nodded. She knew what he was going to say. She had already thought of it.

"You're thinking about Gina's story. About waking up in her father's car."

"It's exactly the same," Ryan said. He sounded glum. "But . . ."

"But where's Alicia?" Debra finished.

"Right. Where's Alicia?" He sighed in frustration. "I just can't figure this. Did Alicia say anything to you? About maybe going somewhere? Or . . ." His voice trailed off.

Debra was hardly listening. Her mind was replaying conversations she'd had with Alicia.

"Ryan . . . did Alicia ever tell you about Tracy? About Jackson Field?"

He frowned. "What do you mean? What about Tracy?"

Debra sipped her coffee. Alicia's crazy story didn't seem so funny anymore.

"What about Tracy?" Ryan asked again.

Debra told him the story.

He stared at her. "You're putting me on, right?"

"Hey, don't look at me that way. I'm just telling you what Alicia told me."

"That doesn't sound like Alicia."

"Sure doesn't. I didn't even take her seriously." Debra leaned back in her seat. "But now . . ."

"But now what?"

Debra shrugged. "I don't know."

Ryan met her eyes. "You're thinking that I drove to Jackson Field? The way Alicia said Tracy did?"

"It's . . . a possibility. I guess."

"That's crazy, Deb. Wouldn't I remember driving somewhere?"

She looked at him. "Do you remember going out to your car?"

Ryan didn't reply. He had a head full of questions, but no answers.

"Besides," Debra said, "Tracy didn't remember."

"Even if Alicia's story is true," Ryan said, "she and Tracy came back together. I was alone in the car."

"I know . . ."

They locked eyes, sharing the same thought.

"Which leaves us where?" Ryan said.

"We could wait around to see if she calls. Or, maybe . . ."

"Take a ride?"

"That's what I was thinking," Deb said. "It beats sitting around and doing nothing."

"We don't even know what we're looking for," Ryan said.

"Funny . . . that's pretty much what I said to Alicia."

A handful of people were scattered about Jackson Field. A man was tossing a frisbee to his dog. A young couple was playing ball with their three young children. Two teens were riding mountain bikes.

Debra led Ryan in the direction that Alicia had taken her a few days before.

"This is a big field, Deb," he said after walking around for a while.

"Tell me something I don't know." She felt as frustrated as he did. Alicia had told her to search for "anything unusual." She hadn't known what to look for then. And she didn't know now.

"Mommy! Mommy! Look!" It was one of the three kids. He was about five, with long curly hair.

Debra and Ryan glanced over. The boy was a few yards away. He was holding up something black.

The boy's mother walked over. She was about thirty. She had the same curly hair as her son.

"What did you find, Mikey?"

"A flashlight! Can I keep it?"

The mother looked it over. "I guess." She gave it back to him.

Debra came closer. "Excuse me. May I see that?"

The mother gave her a doubtful look.

"Just for a second," Debra said.

The boy looked at his mother. She nodded. He handed Debra the flashlight.

"It's mine," he reminded her.

"I know. I'll give it right back."

She studied the flashlight. Then she showed it to Ryan. He frowned. *Alicia* was written in pink nail polish on the handle.

Debra returned the flashlight to the boy. "Thanks."

"This is too weird," Ryan said after mother and son had left. "You're trying to tell me that Alicia and I came here last night?"

"I'm not trying to tell you anything. That was Alicia's flashlight. Draw your own conclusions."

Ryan slowly shook his head. He didn't know what to make of any of this.

"Where *is* she?" Ryan said, as much to himself as to Debra.

Debra's eyes searched the wide field.

Chapter 25

Alicia woke with a start. She sat up on the mat and looked around the room. She was still alone.

It was hard to stay awake. At least with Yonte there, she had someone to talk to. Without him, she had only her fear for company. All she could do was stare at the walls. *Solitary confinement*— wasn't that what they called it when prisoners were locked up by themselves? It was a form of punishment.

How long had Yonte been gone? An hour? Two? Three? She couldn't tell. Her only clue was her rumbling stomach. She was hungry.

She wondered what these creatures ate. What if they ate humans? The thought sent a chill through her. Maybe they planned to use Earth as a food source. Maybe their own planet had run out of food, and—

The door slid open. Yonte entered, closing the door behind him.

Alicia stood up. She was relieved to see him. The huge adults—especially Dal—still frightened her.

"We talk more now," he said, coming closer. He carried a black box in one hand, his word screen in another.

"Could I have something to eat first? I'm starving."

He checked his word screen. "Starving?"

She smiled. "I was exaggerating again. I'm just hungry."

Yonte considered this. "Yes. Earth people eat much. I will bring food." He put the black box and the word screen on the table and left the room. The door slid shut behind him.

Alicia waited a moment. Then, curious, she went to the table. Gently, she picked up the word screen. She examined it. The device weighed very little. She held it close and spoke the word "cat." Almost instantly, a symbol appeared on the screen. She said several more words. Each time, the screen displayed one or more symbols.

"Wow," she said. The screen blinked, but no symbols were displayed. Alicia smiled. *No word for* wow, *huh?*

She studied the many symbols arranged in rows below the screen. She touched one. The word *move* appeared on the screen. She touched another. The word *fast* was displayed. She touched both symbols together. *Run, speed, hurry,* and several other words appeared.

Alicia shook her head, amazed. She wondered how much more the device could do.

Make sentences, probably. Form tenses. Who knew what else?

She put down the word screen and picked up the black box. It looked like a large toolbox. It was made of a lightweight metal or plastic material. Carefully, she opened it.

Inside was a flat, gray case, about eight inches square. Next to the case were several rows of cubes. The top of each cube was labeled with symbols. Alicia raised a top and peeked inside. The cube contained many thin, blue squares. Each was about the size of a wallet photo. The squares seemed to be made of plastic.

Alicia closed the box. She had no idea what it was for. But she didn't want Yonte to catch her snooping through his things. She went back to the mat and sat down.

A few minutes later, Yonte returned. He placed a tray on the table.

"Eat."

Alicia came to the table. Yonte sat across from her. The tray held a cup of clear liquid and a large plate. The plate contained what looked like spinach leaves. Next to the leaves were small pieces of something yellow.

Alicia tried the leaves first. Then she ate one of the yellow pieces.

"Do you like the food?" Yonte asked.

The leaves tasted like paper. The yellow pieces were rubbery. The liquid had no flavor. But Alicia was too hungry to care.

"Yes. Thank you."

Yonte kept asking questions as Alicia ate. He was like a sponge. He soaked up every fact and detail she gave him. Finally, he paused.

"Why are you so interested in Earth?" Alicia asked, before he could start again.

"I am a learner," he answered.

"You said that before. What does that mean?"

"Some are chosen to be learners. I am one. Braktor is another. There are others. We are here to learn. Someday we may be leaders. But we must work hard. Much to study. Many lessons."

It was the longest string of English sentences Yonte had spoken. And he had checked his word screen only once. *In a month, he'll be speaking better than me,* Alicia thought.

"But why study Earth?" she asked.

"Earth is . . ." He paused, trying to remember something. "A project."

Alicia nodded. She had used this word when describing her schoolwork to Yonte.

"Is that all Earth is to you?" she asked. "A project?"

Yonte tilted his head to one side. "I do not understand."

"Why don't your leaders—the Three, as you call them—contact Earth?"

"For what . . . purpose?" Yonte asked.

Another word he's added to his vocabulary, Alicia noted.

"So we can learn about one another," she said.

"We know what we need to know," Yonte said.

The reply disturbed Alicia. And scared her. Again she had that feeling of being viewed as some low form of life.

It was ironic, in a way. The aliens' attitude was not so different from that of humans. History was full of examples of one group of people looking down on another. European explorers looked down on Native Americans. Settlers thought themselves better than Indians. Slave owners viewed Africans as little more than property.

Alicia pushed the empty plate aside. "Thanks for bringing the food."

Yonte did not answer. He appeared to be thinking about something. His silence made Alicia uneasy. She had gotten used to Yonte's constant questions. She wondered what would happen to her when he had nothing more to ask.

"Yonte?" She took a deep breath before asking the question. "Will the Three let me go back?"

His green eye focused on her.

"I cannot say."

"You *can* not . . . or you *will* not?"

"I am only a learner," he said.

"But Leddu is your father. And he is one of the Three."

Yonte kept silent.

"Will you ask? Please?"

The request seemed to trouble him. His head moved back and forth. He hissed and clicked.

"I will ask," he said, finally.

"Thank you."

Yonte watched her a moment. Alicia tried to guess what he was thinking. She couldn't.

"What's in the box?" she asked, changing the subject. Yonte hadn't touched the black box since he'd put it down on the table.

"Lessons," he said.

"You mean, like for school?"

"Yes. Much to know. Much to study. Much work to do. Much, much, much."

Alicia couldn't help smiling. Now he sounded like any kid complaining about too much home-work.

"Can I see?"

"See?"

"See what's in the box. Your lessons."

"They are not like your . . . ." He tried to remember the word, but couldn't. He checked his word screen. "Not like your textbooks."

"I'm curious," Alicia said. "I am a learner, too."

Yonte considered this. Alicia could almost read his thoughts: *How could a lowly human call herself a learner?*

Yonte pulled over the black box. "I will show you," he said.

He opened the box and took out the flat, gray case. He touched a symbol. The case opened into an L-shape. Bright dots of light appeared around the edges.

Yonte chose a cube from the box. He opened it and took out one of the blue squares. He slipped it into an opening on the side of the gray case.

Alicia gasped. There before her on the table were the sights and sounds of Washington, D.C.: the White House, the Capitol, Pennsylvania Avenue, the Washington Monument . . . . She saw people walking along the streets. She heard cars honking their horns. The 3-D images were so real she could almost touch them.

"This . . . this is fantastic."

Yonte touched a symbol on the side of the case. Instantly, they were touring the White House. He touched another symbol. Now they were in Congress, listening to a senator.

Alicia shook her head in disbelief.

Yonte pressed another symbol. The sounds of Washington stopped. In their place, a low voice began speaking in the aliens' language.

"What is he saying?" she asked.

"Teaching," Yonte said. "About government."

Alicia was amazed. "Every one of those blue squares has another lesson like this?"

"Every square has many other lessons." He sounded less than overjoyed. He poked a symbol. The teacher's voice stopped. "Science, mathematics, geography, history . . . ."

Alicia smiled. "Much, much, much."

"Yes," Yonte said. He turned off the viewer. "You understand."

"Can I see more?" Alicia asked.

"Another time." He rose from the chair. He gathered up the black box and the word screen. "There are other tasks I must do now."

Alicia stood up to face him. "Yonte . . . when you go, there is nothing for me to do. I am alone. Could you leave your lesson box here? For me to look at?"

Yonte thought about this. "You do not know my language. You could not understand the teacher."

"I can just look. It would help pass the time."

Yonte was uncertain. He moved his head back and forth.

"Imagine if *you* were locked up by yourself," Alicia said. "Wouldn't you want something to do?"

He hesitated. But the argument seemed to sway him. Finally, he put the box and the word screen back down on the table.

"You can look."

He showed her how to use the viewer. He also left the word screen to help her figure out the symbols that worked the device.

"When will you come back?" Alicia asked, as Yonte started for the door.

His green eye studied her. "Why do you ask that?"

"Because . . . well, because I don't feel so alone when you are here."

"You are afraid?" he asked.

"Yes. I am very afraid."

She hoped he would say that there was nothing to fear. That no one would harm her. That soon she could go home.

But Yonte said none of those things. He just watched her a moment longer. Then he silently left the room.

Chapter 26

Yonte carefully cleaned the jar. Then he put it on the shelf beside the others. He grunted and picked up two more jars.

He hated having to clean up. This was one of the biggest science rooms, too. But it was his turn. Doing experiments was fun. But the learners left such a mess. Tables to clear. Equipment to scrub. Tools to put away.

And everything had to be perfect. If not, Dal would be quick to show that he was not pleased.

Yonte wondered how Earth people got by with only two hands. He couldn't imagine it. Tasks would take forever. Some would be impossible. How could you mix three chemicals at once? How could you run devices that have many controls? How could you even pick up a large box?

Earth people. They were so strange. So ugly. So primitive. And so inferior. Everything he had been taught was true.

And yet . . . the Earth female troubled him. She had helped him at the gate. She had not run off like Braktor. She had not tried to escape. Instead, she had stayed to help him.

Dal called Earth people "worthless." But was this the action of a worthless being?

Yes, her mind was slow. Like that of all Earth people. She knew little, understood less. But she did have thoughts and feelings, not unlike his own. And she wanted to learn, just as he did.

Yonte began putting away tools and instruments. He was careful to place each item into the correct box. He knew Dal would check.

Would the Three let him keep the female? he wondered. Maybe he could even put her to use. Surely she could help clean up. Even with only two arms, she could do something. Any task done would be one less for him.

What would be done with all the Earth people, anyway? According to the Three, no decision had yet been made. More research was needed. More experiments with Implant-6.

But that could take a long time. Meanwhile, why couldn't he keep her? She was harmless.

In fact, he even found her entertaining. Yonte did not mind talking with her. Her words often were of interest. She told him things that his lessons did not. Not important things, but still interesting.

Yes. He would ask the Three if he could keep her. If they said yes, he would tell her that she no longer had to be afraid. If they said no . . . well, that would be too bad.

Just as it was too bad that she could never return to Earth.

Chapter 27

The viewer was incredible. *Like magic,* Alicia thought.

Each blue square was a treasure chest of sights and sounds. Trains, planes. Fields of wheat and corn. Hospitals. Military bases. Zoos. Oil fields and nuclear plants. Schools and libraries.

Different squares explored places around the world. The Great Wall of China. A marketplace in Africa. The Andes Mountains. London. Cairo. New Delhi. Antarctica.

Alicia couldn't understand the language of the spoken lessons. But the word screen helped her read some of the labels on cubes and squares. She looked for matches between the symbols on the labels and those set in rows below the screen. If she found a match, she touched the symbol. The screen displayed the English word.

Some symbols had no match. But many did. Alicia translated words like *Animal Life, Food Sources,* and *Transportation.* Sometimes she could translate only part of a label, such as *View of—* or *—Research.*

At first Alicia would watch a long portion of one lesson before moving on to another. But curiosity soon won out. She began to skip around from cube to cube, sampling different lessons.

The range of content was staggering. Alicia saw cities and forests. Oceans and deserts. Skyscrapers and huts. She heard people speaking Spanish and Hebrew and Greek. She saw factory workers, farmers, scientists.

A human would need weeks to study the lessons on one blue square. The entire set of cubes would take years. How much faster could Yonte's mind grasp the information? Alicia wondered. And how many of these cubes was he expected to know? *Much to study*, Yonte had said. *Many lessons.* He wasn't kidding.

Each square she slipped into the viewer was a new adventure. Some sights she recognized. Many more were new to her. For nearly two hours, Alicia lost herself to the viewer. It was a welcome relief from hours of fear.

And then, in one chilling instant, the fear returned. It gripped her like a cold claw.

She had opened a cube near the bottom of the box. She hadn't even tried to read the label. She just took out a square and put it in the viewer.

A new sight appeared on the tabletop. A small laboratory. Clean, well lit. Two adult creatures were bent over a gray worktable. The subject of their experiment lay between them. Close by was a sleek black machine. It reminded Alicia of her dentist's X-ray machine. The front of the machine was equipped with a thin tube.

The two creatures exchanged words. They adjusted the machine. One carefully aimed the tube. The other's hairy fingers handled the controls. The two worked together slowly and calmly. Alicia could see they had done this many times before.

A bright red beam of light suddenly flashed through the air. It stabbed into the subject's head.

Alicia stared, unable to breathe. Her heart pounded.

Chapter 28

Ryan was in his room, reading *Sports Illustrated,* when the phone rang. He was glad for the interruption. His mind had been on Alicia, not baseball.

"Hi, Ryan."

He recognized Debra's voice. He hoped she had good news.

"Did you hear from her?" he asked before she could speak.

"No. And I can't stand this anymore."

"I know what you mean. I've been sitting around all afternoon. I can't concentrate on anything."

"Same here," Debra said. "You know, maybe going to the police isn't such a dumb idea."

"We went through all that this morning, Deb. What's the point? Alicia hasn't been gone long enough to be considered missing. And if we start telling the cops about zombies driving to Jackson Field, they'll think we're nuts."

For a moment, neither of them spoke.

"Let's go back to the field," Debra said suddenly.

"Go back?" Ryan frowned. "What for?"

"Because it's something to do."

"But we've already done that. We know Alicia was there because of the flashlight, even though I don't remember driving her. Why would you want to go back now?"

"I don't mean now. I mean tonight."

"Tonight?" Ryan shook his head. The world seemed to be going crazy. His memory of last night was a blank. Alicia had disappeared. And Debra was making no sense.

"Whatever happened to Tracy happened at night," Debra said. "And whatever happened to you and Alicia happened at night."

"So what are you saying? You want to stake out Jackson Field?"

"Yes."

"But—"

"Maybe we'll see something at night that we didn't see during the day. What have we got to lose?"

Ryan started to object, then stopped. He felt tired and frustrated. But being negative wouldn't help. Debra was right. They had nothing to lose except maybe some sleep.

"All right. Let's do it. How about if I swing by and pick you up?"

"Deal. What time?"

"Nine, nine-thirty?"

"Fine," Debra said. "That'll give me time to figure out something to tell my mother."

Chapter 29

Alicia touched a symbol on the side of the viewer. The scene in the laboratory froze. The two creatures stopped moving. The beam of light hung in the air like a bright red arrow.

Alicia looked closely at the subject on the worktable. He was a dark-skinned boy, maybe 15 years old. Judging from his clothes, he was not from America.

The boy's eyes were closed. The beam of light seemed to be fixed on his left temple.

Alicia touched the viewer again. The scene resumed.

The beam of light remained locked on the boy's head. Both creatures watched carefully. Occasionally, one would touch the controls. The boy never moved.

Alicia's stomach twisted.

What are they doing to him?

Finally, one of the creatures shut off the beam.

The viewer went black. Alicia heard the teacher's recorded voice. She wished she could understand his words.

A moment later, a new scene appeared. A large room. Six or seven adult creatures were seated on one side. Alicia recognized Dal and Leddu. Two other creatures stood nearby. They were the same two who had operated the light machine.

Across the room stood the boy who had been on the table. His back was against the wall. His eyes were wide with terror.

The creatures spoke among themselves. Then one of the standing creatures picked up a small, gray device. It was about the size and shape of a plate. Everyone fell silent. They all looked at the boy.

Alicia could hardly bear to watch. The poor boy was so scared he began to cry. He tried to speak to the creatures. Alicia did not recognize his language. No one answered him. The boy shouted. He was pleading with them. They ignored him.

The creature holding the gray device touched a symbol. Immediately, the boy's body went stiff. It was as if he had gotten an electric shock.

The creature touched other symbols. The boy lurched two steps forward. Then two more. His head jerked from side to side. His body seemed to be out of his control. Even so, he kept on crying and pleading.

Several of the seated creatures spoke. Clearly, they approved.

The boy was sobbing. He seemed to be trying to back away. But his legs wouldn't move.

The creature touched the device again. The boy took another step forward. Then another.

And then, suddenly, he screamed. Both hands clutched his head. His whole body shuddered.

Then he collapsed to the floor.

Alicia gasped. She felt sick.

Dal, Leddu, and the others were all on their feet now. The creature with the device poked several symbols. Everyone was talking at once.

The boy didn't move.

The viewer went black again.

Alicia stared at the blackness. She heard the teacher's voice. But the words sounded far away. Her mind was numb with horror.

A few seconds later, another scene appeared. At first, Alicia thought it was the same one being repeated. She saw the same large room. Once again six or seven adult creatures were seated, watching. The same two creatures were on their feet. One held the gray device.

But this time there was a young Asian girl across the room. She was about the same age as Alicia. Her pretty face was pale with fear.

Oh God, no. Not again.

Alicia wanted to turn the viewer off. But she couldn't. She felt like a witness to a bloody car accident. She didn't want to look. But she couldn't turn away.

The creature worked the device. The girl's

body stiffened. Like the boy, she too was crying. But she said hardly a word. Alicia guessed she was too scared to talk.

The girl staggered forward a few steps. Then she turned and walked a few more steps. Her head jerked to one side. Tears ran down her cheeks. She stopped. Moved forward. Stopped again. Her body swayed from side to side.

Many of the observers were speaking. Dal made a comment to the creature holding the device. Leddu kept his dark green eye on the girl.

They had the girl walk from one end of the room to the other. Then back again. She seemed to be a prisoner in her own body. Her hands twitched.

Everyone in the room seemed very pleased.

And then it happened again. The girl let out a sudden shriek. Her hands flew to her head. Her body shook.

And she collapsed.

Dal was on his feet. He snarled at the creature holding the device. Some of the others also shouted angry words.

Alicia didn't look at the creatures. She was staring at the girl's lifeless body on the floor.

Blood trickled from one ear.

Chapter 30

Yonte took his seat on the far left side of the assembly room. This was the learners' section. Braktor sat beside him. A dozen other young learners also sat in the section.

Braktor was quiet. She was sulking. Dal had punished her for her behavior at the gate. She felt angry and embarrassed. Several learners had made fun of her. This made her mad at Yonte. It was easier to blame Yonte than blame herself. Yonte shouldn't have gotten caught in the gate. He was always making her look bad. Always showing off how much he knew. He was too smart for his own good. And that interfering Earth female! Braktor was angry at her, too. Had that worthless alien not come, none of this would have happened.

The adults were slowly filling the rows of chairs in the assembly room. They hissed and clicked as they entered. They spoke quietly among themselves, much like humans in a court-room. More than fifty adults came into the room.

The Three entered last: Dal, Leddu, and Nemm. Nemm was as big as the others, but she was female. Like other females, her eye color was yellow.

The Three took their seats in the front of the room. The door to the assembly room was closed. Latecomers were not permitted to enter.

The room fell silent.

After a moment, Nemm rose from her chair. It was her turn to speak first.

"My greeting to you," she said, speaking in her native language. "This meeting of the Three begins."

For the next two hours, different creatures gave reports. They talked about food production and water supplies. About adding more solar cells. About systems that needed repair. About ongoing research and planned experiments. They discussed various problems and possible solutions.

Members of the audience addressed questions to the Three. They took turns answering. Often the Three would confer before one of them answered.

One member of the audience spoke at a time. When one creature finished talking, he or she would sit down. Then another would speak. Rarely did one speaker interrupt another. Only the adults in the audience spoke. The learners kept silent.

After the reports, Leddu rose.

"We move on to the next topic: the Earth Project. We are—"

A creature in the third row stood up. He waited to be recognized.

Leddu paused and looked at him. "Kanir?"

"A question. I have heard that an alien entered the station. An alien that we had not called. Is this true?"

"Yes. A young Earth female traveled the light."

"How is this possible?" Kanir asked.

"A chance event," Leddu answered. "Of no concern."

Another creature stood.

"Jaq?"

"I have heard that the alien injured Yonte. Is this true?"

Yonte wanted to speak. But he knew better than to interrupt. Braktor looked down at her feet. She wished she were somewhere else.

"No," Leddu said. He hesitated. "In truth, the Earth female helped my son."

The audience buzzed. They had never heard such a thing.

Leddu briefly explained what had happened at the gate. He cast no blame on Braktor.

The audience buzzed more loudly. Help from an alien? *Impossible,* said one creature. *Very amusing,* said another.

In the learners' section, a young male called an insult in Braktor's direction. Braktor pretended not to hear. She was already in enough trouble. She didn't want to call any more attention to herself. She would deal with the male later.

"Silence!" Leddu commanded the room.

The talking stopped.

"If you have questions, ask them. We will answer as best we can. Whispers and rumors serve no purpose."

A creature rose in the back. He was older than most of the others.

"Yes, Surdnon?"

"Has the alien been destroyed?"

"No," Leddu replied.

"But she came without being called."

"That is correct."

"So her memory was not blocked."

Leddu glanced at Yonte. "That is also correct."

Surdnon tilted his head to one side. "I do not understand. If the alien's memory was not blocked . . . ."

Nemm rose. She spoke quietly first to Leddu, then to Dal. Leddu sat down.

"The matter is not yet decided," Nemm told the questioner.

Surdnon seemed surprised. "Not decided?"

"The Three have not reached agreement."

"But how so?" Surdnon asked.

Nemm spoke again with Leddu and Dal before answering.

"Dal votes that we destroy the alien. Leddu keeps silent for now."

142

"And you?" Surdnon asked. "What is your vote?"

"Like Leddu, I am silent for now."

Surdnon fluttered a hand in the air. "Dal is right. Destroy her."

Several other audience members muttered agreement.

Yonte slowly rose to his feet. He was tense. Learners seldom spoke at meetings unless they were spoken to first.

Nemm silenced the room. She fixed her yellow eye on Yonte.

"The son of Leddu wishes to speak?"

"Yes." Yonte felt everyone's eyes on him. He hesitated. His head moved nervously back and forth.

"Well, speak then," Nemm ordered.

"I . . . I wish to keep her," he said softly.

Braktor and some of the other learners looked at him in disbelief.

"What?" Nemm said. "Speak up!"

"I said, I wish to keep her."

Nemm looked at Yonte much the same way that Braktor had. The audience began to buzz again.

"And why is that?" Nemm demanded.

Yonte tried to explain.

Around the room, creatures exchanged comments. Hands fluttered in the air. Nemm had to call out twice for silence.

"Sit down," one of the learners whispered to Yonte. "You'll make the Three angry."

143

But Yonte remained standing. He did not think his request unreasonable. He had a right to wait for an answer.

Yonte already knew that the female would not be allowed to go back to Earth. If the Three would not let him keep her, she would be destroyed.

Nemm spoke with Leddu and Dal. Yonte could see that the two disagreed. This was not unusual. He knew his father to be fair and reasonable. But Dal saw only one point of view: his own.

Nemm turned toward Yonte again.

"Dal votes to destroy the alien. Leddu votes to let you keep the alien for a set time." Nemm paused, thinking.

Yonte waited. Nemm had the deciding vote. Yonte knew it could go either way. Nemm was more open-minded than Dal. But allowing a learner to keep an alien had never been done before.

"This matter requires more thought than I have given it," Nemm said. "I will cast my vote at the next meeting. For now, the Earth female remains where she is."

Yonte sat down. He saw Leddu looking at him. His father appeared pleased. What Yonte had done had taken courage.

"Now," Nemm continued. "We move on to the Earth Project."

Chapter 31

Alicia sat on the mat, trying to calm down. She took long, slow breaths. She focused on relaxing her muscles.

But she couldn't wipe the images from her mind.

The terrified teenagers.

The horrible screams.

The blood trickling from the young girl's ear.

Alicia knew she had to go back to the viewer. The blue squares held the answers to her questions. Answers that the creatures would probably never give her. Answers that she might never know if Yonte took the viewer away.

But the thought of seeing more of what she had already seen turned her stomach.

Alicia sat for several more minutes. Finally, she rose and walked back to the table. Her legs felt shaky.

She picked up the cube from which she had taken the awful blue square. She looked at the cube's label. She hadn't bothered to try to read it before. She did now.

Using the word screen, she was able to translate the second part of the label, but not the first: —*Project*. She removed the blue square from the viewer and examined its label. Again, she could not get the first part. But the second part was a number: *1*.

She took the other squares out of the cube. Many of their labels had the same first part, but different second parts. The second parts were a sequence of numbers, from 2 through 6.

Alicia chose the square labeled —*3*. She took a deep breath and slipped the square into the viewer.

The laboratory again. The worktable. The black machine and red beam of light. Two adults creatures bent over another human subject. These were not the same adults as on the other square. But the process was the same.

The viewer went black. Alicia heard a different teacher's voice. Then the other room appeared again. The same room in which she had seen—

Alicia stopped the viewer. Her heart pounded. She wanted to fling the viewer across the room. Smash it to bits. Never look at another gruesome image.

But she couldn't do that.

She forced herself to turn the viewer on again.

This time the subject was a blond-haired teen. He looked about 18. He wasn't crying. But like the others, he stared at the creatures with terror-filled eyes.

A different creature worked the control device this time. The teen's body stiffened. But he didn't move. The creature holding the device spoke to the seated onlookers. Dal, Leddu, and the others listened, but said nothing.

Then an odd thing happened. The creature with the device spoke to the teen in English.

"Go there," the creature said. He pointed to one side of the room.

The teen hesitated, then did as told.

"Walk there," the creature ordered. He pointed to the opposite wall.

The teen did so.

The creature spoke again to the onlookers.

"Now walk back again," the creature told the teen.

The teen began walking back to the other wall. He was halfway there when the creature touched a symbol on his device.

Immediately, the teen stopped. His eyes were open, but his face was blank.

The creature worked his device. The teen resumed walking. The creature touched a symbol. Again, the teen froze.

The onlookers watched with interest. Leddu asked a question. Two other creatures made comments. The creatures in the room discussed what they had seen.

All the while, the teen remained as frozen as a statue.

Then the viewer went black.

Before the next scene could appear, Alicia removed the blue square. She picked up a different square. This one was labeled —5. She put it into the viewer.

The same room again. But now there were more than a dozen spectators. And there were more subjects.

Instead of just one frightened boy or girl, there were five. All were in their teens. They huddled together. Two held hands. One was weeping.

The creature with the control device pointed to the far wall. The five teens slowly began walking. The creature touched a symbol on the device. Instantly, three of the teens froze. A fourth took two more steps, then halted. But the fifth—a tall boy in jeans—seemed unaffected.

When the others stopped, the boy hesitated. He looked around. He appeared confused. The boy raised a hand to his head. He was clearly in some pain.

Then one of the frozen teens, a red-haired girl, began to twitch. A moment later, she sank to her knees.

The creature with the control device was not pleased. But the onlookers were impressed. Even Dal made what sounded like a positive comment.

The red-haired girl struggled to stand. She couldn't. One arm began to shake. Then she—

Alicia turned off the viewer. She rubbed her eyes. She just couldn't watch anymore.

This was all a nightmare.

How long had these experiments been going on? A year? Two years? Five? Longer than that?

How many people had these creatures taken for their "project"?

How many had they killed?

Where is Ryan? Alicia had asked Leddu.

There are many rooms, the creature had replied. *Many Ry-ans.*

At that moment, Alicia would have given anything to have Ryan beside her. But she didn't even know where he was.

Or what they had done to him.

She pushed that awful thought out of her mind. But in its place came a question. A question just as awful—

What will they do to me?

Chapter 32

In the assembly room, the Earth Project reports had begun. As always, they would go on for some time.

Braktor leaned closer to Yonte. "Talking to aliens . . ." she whispered. "You must be an even bigger fool than I thought."

"Strong words from someone who runs from gates," Yonte replied.

Braktor let out a low growl. "I went for help."

"You ran off like a *crixen,*" Yonte said. On their home planet, a crixen was a small, ugly, six-legged creature. It was afraid of everything.

The remark made Braktor furious. But she held herself back. The Three did not look kindly at learners who quarreled during a meeting.

"I am no crixen," she shot back.

"No," Yonte whispered. "You have only two legs."

Braktor was fuming. Yonte always thought he was so clever. Well, she could be just as clever. She would find a way to get even.

Dal glanced in their direction. Instantly, their whispering stopped.

An older creature named Hukolf was reporting now. Hukolf was a scientist. He led the group working on Implant-6. Hukolf spoke in very technical language. Even so, every adult in the room understood him. Even the learners understood most of what he had to say.

When Hukolf finished, he remained standing. He looked at the Three. He was ready to answer questions.

Leddu spoke first. "What is the rate of success now for Implant-6?"

"Almost 40 percent total success. About 25 percent partial success. These are estimates, of course."

"And the rest?" Nemm asked.

Hukolf hesitated. The Three did not like bad news.

"About 25 percent failure . . . 10 percent loss."

"That is poor," Dal said.

"It is better," Hukolf replied quietly.

"*Better?*" Dal snapped. "Not even half the Implant-6 devices are fully successful. More than one in three fail completely or kill the subjects. You call this *better?*"

Hukolf shifted his feet. "Better than Implant-5. Far better than Implant-4."

Dal's hands fluttered. "Progress comes too slowly, Hukolf."

"Speak more of partial success," Leddu said. "How partial?"

Hukolf's discomfort grew. "Some interference

with memory and brain activity," he said to Leddu. "Some effect on personality. Some . . . other problems."

"Be specific," Leddu prompted.

Hukolf's head moved back and forth. He avoided Dal's cold gaze. "Implant-6 is better able to immobilize than to control."

"This *again?*" Dal growled. "Why must we hear this same thing over and over?"

"Dal, it is far easier to stop the brain than to control it," Hukolf tried to explain. "Even the brain of an Earth being. It will take more time."

"Excuses!" Dal snarled.

Hukolf kept silent.

"Any sign of discovery?" Nemm asked.

Hukolf brightened. "None. The Earth people suspect nothing. And even if they did, our work is virtually undetectable by their primitive technology."

"And the homing disks," Leddu said. "They continue to function well?"

"Yes. Very well."

Dal leaned forward in his chair. "Why is it, Hukolf, that the homing disks succeed but Implant-6 does not?"

Hukolf met Dal's dark eye. "A homing disk is simple. It attaches from outside. It does only two things: block the memory and draw in the subject. It functions for only a short time. Implant-6 is far more complex and powerful. It must be fixed inside the brain. And it is permanent."

"More excuses," Dal said. "We already know all this."

"Can you estimate time?" Nemm asked. "How much longer before the success rate reaches 90 percent?"

"Success measured by control," Dal added. "Not just stopping the brain."

"Ninety percent?" Hukolf repeated. He looked more uncomfortable than ever. He wasn't sure they would ever reach 90 percent. But he would not admit that.

"I cannot say," the scientist answered.

"We ask only for an estimate," Dal said. "Surely you can manage that."

Leddu turned toward Dal. "If he cannot say, he cannot say."

"But he is Implant-6 group leader," Dal replied.

"Would you have him make up a number?" Leddu said. He respected Dal. But sometimes Dal's demands were unreasonable.

"The group leader should know," Dal answered.

"There is no point to debating this," Nemm said. "Group leader or not, Hukolf cannot say what he does not know."

"Then perhaps it is time for Hukolf to step aside," Dal said.

Hukolf looked at Leddu for support. But Leddu's patience with the scientist, too, was starting to wear thin. The Implant experiments had been going on almost as long as his son had been alive. Yet, as Dal had said, progress came slowly.

"That is a matter for the Three to discuss," Leddu said.

"Agreed," said Dal.

"Agreed," said Nemm.

Hukolf silently returned to his seat. He had no desire to argue with the Three. Let them choose another group leader if they wanted to. He had not been the first. He knew he would not be the last.

Chapter 33

After the meeting of the Three, Braktor went to her room. She had lessons to study.

But her mind was not on her lessons. Her mind was on Yonte.

A crixen, he had called her. Yonte, with his clever mouth. Yonte, who was always showing her up. He thought he was special just because his father was one of the Three.

Well, he was *not* special. And this time she would show *him* something. She would teach clever Yonte a lesson.

Her plan was simple. Simple, yet perfect. It would make Yonte look bad. And it would get rid of that interfering Earth female.

Yonte had told her where the female was being kept. All Braktor had to do was let the alien get out.

Just think of Dal's reaction! An alien running loose in the station! Dal was already angry when he first found her here. At the meeting, he voted to destroy her. But the decision was delayed.

This only made him angrier. And now the whole station would have to be searched to catch her again.

Dal would explode! *How did she get out?* he would roar. And Braktor would be happy to tell him:

Yonte must have forgotten to close the door. How else?

Careless, careless Yonte.

As for the Earth female, escaping would seal her fate. Nemm would be sure to cast her vote with Dal. Even Leddu would agree. *So much fuss over one Earth creature?* Leddu would say. *A waste of time. Destroy her at once.*

So the worthless alien would be destroyed. And Yonte would feel the fury of Dal.

Yes, it was a perfect plan.

Chapter 34

When Yonte returned, Alicia was sitting on the floor. She was leaning against a wall. She did not get up.

Something had changed. Yonte could sense it. He glanced at the table. The viewer was open, but turned off. Several blue frames lay scattered about. He looked at Alicia.

"My lessons did not interest you?" he asked.

Alicia met Yonte's large green eye. The screams of teenagers still echoed in her mind. She saw again the blood trickling from the young girl's ear.

She rose slowly to her feet. As great as Alicia's fear was, her anger was even greater.

"Your lessons made me sick," she said.

Yonte's head tilted to the side.

"I do not understand."

Alicia's eyes flashed. "How long, Yonte? How long have you been experimenting with Earth people?" She stepped closer. Her voice rose. "How many have you terrorized? How many have you crippled? How many have you *killed?*" She was almost shouting now. "Did you kill Ryan, too? Will you kill me next?"

Yonte stared at her. The Earth female's anger fascinated him. Such strong feelings from a lower life-form.

Her words surprised him, though. How could she know of the Earth experiments?

But as soon as the question entered his mind, Yonte knew the answer. He picked up the open cube from the table. He read the label: *Earth Project.*

Yonte let out a growl. *Foolish!* His head moved rapidly back and forth. Two arms swiped the air. How could he have left the *Earth Project* cube in his lesson box? The cube that held the history of the Implant series. If his father found out, punishment would be swift and harsh. And if Dal heard . . . . Yonte didn't even want to imagine that.

"You should not have viewed those lessons," Yonte said, calming himself.

"Why not?" Alicia shot back. "Those are my people you've been torturing."

"Torturing?" Yonte did not know the word. He took the word screen from the table and repeated the word into it. He looked at the screen. The meaning puzzled him.

"I do not understand. We are not . . . torturing."

"No? What do you call it? Shooting light rays into people's heads. Moving people around like

158

puppets. Frying their brains."

Yonte kept silent. He watched her, trying to understand. No one had ever questioned the Earth Project.

"You don't care, do you?" Alicia said. "Earth people mean nothing to you, do they?"

Yonte thought for a long time. Finally, he answered with a question of his own.

"Are your scientists so different from ours?"

"What are you talking about?"

"Your scientists do research. They do experiments. Many creatures are used in these experiments. Many suffer. Many die."

Alicia looked at him in disbelief. "You're talking about . . . laboratory animals? Rats and mice? Guinea pigs? Monkeys? Is *that* how you view us?"

Yonte hissed and clicked. The Earth female understood so little.

"The universe is large," he said. "There are many creatures. Each creature is superior to another."

"And superior creatures can do whatever they want to the others?"

"Is it not so on Earth?" Yonte said. "Not only scientists. All Earth people. They eat other creatures. They use their body parts for clothing. They force them to pull heavy loads. They make them—"

"Animals," Alicia interrupted. "Those are *animals,* Yonte."

Yonte's head tilted. He gave Alicia a long look. "And you? Are you not yourself an animal?"

"But . . ." Alicia searched for a reply. "But we have reasons. Food. Shelter. Survival."

"And we have reasons, too," he said.

Alicia hesitated. She was afraid to ask. But she had to.

"What . . . what reasons?"

Yonte weighed his answer. There was no point to keeping silent. The female would either be destroyed or not. Even if she was not destroyed, she would still not be allowed to return to Earth.

"Look to your own history," he said. "Think of your school lessons. Why do explorers set out? For land. For riches. Sometimes for slaves. It is not difficult to understand."

Alicia's throat was so dry, she could hardly swallow.

"You want . . . the planet?"

"The universe is vast. But there are not many planets such as yours. Earth is large. It has many resources. There is much water. The climate is mild."

Alicia's legs felt weak. She sat down in a chair.

"You want the planet," she repeated to herself, trying to grasp the words.

"Is this so surprising?" Yonte asked. "As large as our own planet is, it is still limited."

Alicia shook her head. "It's not at all what we imagined . . . ."

"I do not understand."

"In the movies . . . usually flying saucers attack the Earth."

"We have no wish to turn the planet into a battleground. That would not serve our purpose."

Alicia looked up at him. She felt numb inside.

"And the people, Yonte?" she asked softly. "What will happen to the people?"

"That I cannot yet say."

Alicia ran a hand through her hair. She took a deep breath.

"You're never going to let me go back, are you?"

Yonte held her gaze. He had expected the question.

"No."

Alicia felt a hard lump in her throat. Tears welled up in her eyes. She fought them back. But a single tear rolled down her cheek.

"What will you do with me?"

Yonte saw her sadness, her fear. Her distress touched him. Strangely, he had come to like this Earth female. But there was nothing he could do.

"The Three have not decided," he said.

Alicia brushed the tear from her cheek. She stared down at her trembling hands. For a moment, she and Yonte were both silent. Then Alicia looked up.

"Why only teenagers?" she asked. Her voice was just above a whisper.

"I do not understand."

"The experiments I saw . . . I was wondering

why all the people were young."

"Progress has been greatest with young subjects. The work with adults has been more difficult. But that too will succeed. In time."

"In time," Alicia echoed glumly. She wondered just how much time Earth had left.

"Behavior is also a factor," Yonte added as an afterthought.

"What do you mean?"

"Young people's behavior is changeable. Often odd. Subjects we return to Earth sometimes exhibit side effects."

"Effects that are less noticeable among teens."

"That is correct. You understand."

"Yes . . . too well." She rubbed her eyes. She felt utterly drained. But there was one more question she had to ask.

"How many . . . 'subjects' have been returned to Earth?"

Yonte considered.

"I cannot say for sure. Too many to count easily."

Chapter 35

Debra reached over to grab another soda from the backseat of Ryan's Ford. "Do you want one?" she asked.

Ryan didn't answer. He was slouched in the driver's seat, his head against the headrest. He was staring into space.

"Hello? Anybody home?"

Ryan blinked and looked at her.

"Sorry. I was thinking."

"About Alicia?"

"What else?"

They had been sitting in the car outside Jackson Field for more than an hour. They had seen and heard absolutely nothing.

"Hang in there, Ryan." Debra tried to sound more cheerful than she felt. "She'll turn up."

"Alicia would have called . . . if she could."

Debra did not reply. She knew he was right.

"What if something—"

"Please, Ryan. Don't start with the what-ifs. There's no point."

"Oh, like there's really a point to sitting here?" he said irritably.

"You want to go?"

He hesitated, then shook his head.

"No. Sitting around at home is worse."

They were both quiet a moment. Then Ryan looked up.

"I'm sorry, Deb. I guess I'm lousy company tonight. I'm just frustrated. And worried."

She touched his arm. "I know, Ryan. Me too."

They sat in silence for a while.

"Want to walk?" Ryan asked, shifting in his seat. "I'm getting stiff."

"Sure."

Debra handed him one of the flashlights they had brought. She took the other. They got out of the car.

Chapter 36

Never to return home.

Never to see her mother again.

Or Ryan. Or Deb.

The thought was too awful for Alicia to bear.

After Yonte had gone, Alicia tried to collect herself. She paced back and forth in the small room. She fought the panic building inside her.

At first, a part of her would not accept the truth. *Could* not accept it. But that first wave of disbelief passed. A second wave washed over her, a wave of anger.

How could these creatures treat Earth this way? As though the entire planet was theirs for the taking. As though all the people were worthless. How dare they? Superior or not, they had no right to do what they were doing. No right at all. They were arrogant, smug, heartless beings. All their knowledge and power couldn't change that.

But in the silent emptiness of the room, Alicia's anger slowly faded. A new emotion took its place. An emotion as cold and unforgiving as Dal's dark eye. Alicia felt despair.

She was trapped. This room was her jail cell. The only way out was a single door, which was always kept shut. She had no hope of overpowering the creatures and trying to escape. They were far too strong for her. And even if she could get past them, then what? She was on a space station millions of miles from Earth.

Even before Yonte had said so, Alicia had known the creatures would never let her go. How could they? She knew what they were doing. She knew what they intended to do. She posed a risk to their plans.

They would surely kill her. But not before experimenting on her. Just like those poor kids she had seen in Yonte's viewer. Maybe she'd be the next victim on the floor, blood flowing from her ear.

Alicia sat down at the table. She buried her face in her hands. She felt the wetness on her cheeks. She wished she were somewhere else. Anywhere else. She wished that—

The door suddenly slid open. Alicia's stomach froze. She looked up, expecting the worst. Dal coming to take her away. Or maybe Leddu. She hoped Yonte would be there too, so she wouldn't feel so alone.

She watched the doorway.

No one appeared.

Alicia waited, staring through the open doorway.

No one came in.

She listened for sounds, voices. For hissing and clicking.

Only silence.

Slowly, Alicia rose to her feet. She walked to the doorway.

She looked into the corridor.

No one there.

She frowned. This didn't make sense. *Someone* must have opened the door from outside.

She waited. Listening. Watching.

Nothing.

Could Yonte be offering her a chance to escape? Not likely. He was far too respectful of the adults to do such a thing. And much too afraid of Dal.

Yet, here she was, facing an open door.

A malfunction? Yes, that must be it. Some sort of short circuit in the door. Like when the gate had gone crazy and closed on Yonte.

And if that was the case, this door too might close again any second. If she was going to act, she had to act now.

Alicia did not hesitate. She had nothing to lose. If the creatures caught her, they'd kill her. If she stayed, they'd kill her anyway.

She ran to the table and grabbed the word screen. Thank God Yonte had left it. Without it, she had no hope of ever understanding the aliens' symbols.

She walked rapidly down the corridor. Her heart pounded. She knew this was her one and only chance.

She had to find an "elevator" to get back to the corridor where she'd arrived. There had to be more than just one. But she had no time to search. She had to retrace her steps, and do it fast.

She wondered if the creatures had already fixed the gate. If so, she'd have to get it open as she did before, when Yonte had been trapped. She prayed that wouldn't be necessary. There was no time.

She moved quickly, glancing into rooms she passed. Every few steps, she looked over her shoulder. She listened for any sound.

She rounded a corner. Up ahead, she could see the gate.

It was still open.

Lucky break, Alicia thought. She quickened her pace. She hoped her luck would hold.

She passed the gate and followed the corridor around to the right. She tried to remember how far it was to—

Clicks and hisses.

Alicia froze. She flattened herself against a wall.

From which direction had the sounds come? Ahead? Behind?

She waited, listening.

Voices.

Getting louder.

Coming toward her.

Hide! her mind screamed.

She ducked into the nearest open room. In the dim light, it appeared to be a large storage room. She pressed her back to the wall.

The voices were getting louder.

If they're coming here, I'm dead.

Hisses and clicks.

Alicia held her breath.

Two, maybe three, creatures were right outside now. Their hoarse, whispery voices sent a chill through her.

Could they hear her heart thumping?

The seconds passed so slowly, Alicia wanted to scream.

Then the voices began to fade.

They're going past . . .

She waited an extra minute before she would let herself breath again. Then she peeked outside.

The creatures were gone.

Alicia hurried down the corridor. All her senses were on high alert. She was ready for any sound, any movement.

She remembered that the "elevator" had a wide metal door. She had to be getting close now. Her eyes scanned the corridor ahead.

Come on, come on. Where is it?

She didn't remember walking this far when they'd brought her.

Maybe I went right past it. Maybe I'm going the wrong way—

But, suddenly, there it was. Straight ahead.

Alicia rushed forward. There was a circle on the wall beside the door. She touched it, and the door opened. Alicia stepped inside.

She looked at the control panel. There were six different symbols. If she touched the wrong one, she might send herself right back to the aliens.

She raised the word screen. She tried to match the symbols on the control panel with the ones beneath the screen. But her hand was shaking badly. She could hardly read the small symbols.

Pull yourself together! Concentrate! One symbol at a time . . . .

Alicia held the word screen with both hands to steady it. She studied the symbols.

There! A match!

She touched the symbol on the word screen. The screen instantly displayed an English word: *Supplies.*

Alicia kept looking. She found another match. She touched the symbol. The screen translated: *Food preparation.*

Alicia bit her lip, kept searching.

She found a third match, touched the symbol. *Energy.*

Oh come on!

She took a deep breath, tried to calm herself. Three symbols left on the control panel. It had to be one of them.

But they looked so much alike. It was hard to find an exact match.

Focus! she told herself.

Her head was throbbing. Symbols danced before her eyes. She tried to study them one at a ti—

Wait! There! Another match.

The screen blinked: *Communications.*

No! She cursed in frustration.

Two symbols left.

Alicia rubbed her eyes. She kept looking.

Hisses and clicks.

Oh no—

Someone was coming. Her time had run out.

She stared at the two remaining symbols.

Fifty-fifty chance, she thought.

Hisses and clicks, getting louder.

Alicia jabbed one of the symbols. The door closed.

There was a flash of light.

The door opened again.

A large, open area. Shiny black tables and chairs. Machines. Bright green lights. Several adult creatures standing and talking.

NO! This isn't it!

Alicia's finger shot out for the one remaining symbol on the control panel.

But in the instant before the door closed again, one creature glanced up.

And looked straight at her.

Chapter 37

Yonte stood in the corridor. He stared into the empty room. It was not possible. Yet, the Earth female was gone.

He had come back to speak with her again. To do what he could to ease her fear. There was another reason, too. The word she had used—*torture*—disturbed him. He had no wish to make her or any creature suffer. The Implant experiments were done only because they had to be.

Yonte was not sure why it mattered to him that the Earth female understand this. After all, she was but a low form of alien life. Still, she had worth. More worth than Yonte had been led to expect.

But . . . she was gone. She had gotten out and was loose somewhere in the station.

How this could have happened, Yonte did not know. What he did know was that the Three would be furious. He had best tell his father at once. If Dal found out first—

Yonte heard a sound close by. He turned and saw his father approaching rapidly. He did not look pleased.

"Is it true?" Leddu demanded. He spoke in their native language.

Yonte was confused. He had only just discovered the alien's disappearance himself. How could his father already know?"

"Is it true? Leddu repeated more loudly.

"The Earth female has gotten out. Yes. But how did you—"

Leddu's green eye flashed. "How did she get out?"

Yonte took a step back.

"I . . . do not know."

"It is said that you left the door open."

Yonte looked up at his father in horror. Such an error would be serious. *Very* serious.

"That is not true. I would not be so foolish. Who said this?"

"You were the only one to go to the alien. Is that not so?"

Yonte's head moved back and forth. He looked down at the floor.

"Yes," he said quietly. "I was the only one."

"And the alien could not have opened the door herself. True?"

"Yes."

"And except for the adults who brought her, no one else even knew where the alien was. True?"

Yonte hesitated.

"True?" Leddu repeated.

Yonte met his eye.

"No. Not true."

Leddu waited, but Yonte did not go on.

"Well? Speak!"

"I do not want to blame anyone. But I did not leave the door open. I would not do that."

Leddu watched his son carefully. Yonte's voice was firm. He held his head high. Never before had his son spoken falsely. Leddu did not think he spoke falsely now.

"Who else knew?" Leddu asked, softening his tone.

Yonte looked down. He kept silent.

"Did you tell the learners, Yonte?"

Yonte could not escape his father's gaze.

"I told only one other."

"Who?

Yonte hissed and clicked.

"Who?"

"Braktor."

Leddu considered this. The competition between his son and Braktor was well known. Could Braktor have freed the alien, then blamed Yonte?

Leddu did not know. But he would find out.

"You are certain that you closed the door?" Leddu asked.

"I am certain."

Leddu held his gaze a moment longer. Then he turned away.

"We will speak more later. I go to talk with Dal and Nemm."

Yonte watched his father stride down the corridor.

Had Braktor purposely let the alien out? Yonte knew it was possible. Braktor was smart. But her judgment was often poor. And she had too much spite.

If Braktor had indeed done this, she would learn a hard lesson. More than likely, the Three would send her home. The worst punishment of all.

In an odd way, Yonte would miss her. But not too much.

And what of the Earth female? Where could she go?

How scared she must be to run blindly off. How desperate she must feel. But Yonte could understand. It was every creature's basic instinct. To stay alive. To fight for survival. In her place, Yonte would have done the same.

He started walking slowly down the corridor. He tried to sort through the emotions he felt. Anger at Braktor, if she was behind this. Fear of the Three, if they did not believe him. And a third emotion. One that surprised him.

Sadness.

Sadness for the alien.

Chapter 38

The creature had seen her. Alicia was certain. It had stared right at her before the "elevator" door closed.

Another flash of light.

The door opened again.

Alicia was afraid to look. If this wasn't the right corridor—

But it was. Or, at least, it appeared to be. There was no way of knowing if all the corridors looked alike.

Alicia stepped out. She glanced in both directions.

The corridor was empty.

Thank God.

She tried to recall from which direction she'd come.

From the left. Yes, she was sure of it.

She hurried down the corridor, clutching the word screen.

How quickly would the word spread? Would the creatures sound an alarm? Were they already searching for her?

Alicia followed the curve of the corridor. She moved as fast as caution would allow. Hurrying along, she glanced into open rooms, but saw no one. She wondered if anyone was inside the closed rooms.

Alicia knew she had to be nearing the place where she'd first met the creatures. She only hoped none of them was around now.

There. That room. Wasn't that where she'd seen the five creatures gathered around the table?

Alicia slowed. She listened for any sounds. For hisses and clicks.

All was silent.

She kept going.

Yes. This was the room. She could see the large, circular black table.

She remembered her utter shock when she'd first seen the creatures. Shock and total disbelief. The dense hair. The arms. The big green eye. Her horror as all five creatures came toward her. Her first terrifying sight of the huge Dal . . . .

Alicia broke into run.

She had to get back to Earth. *Had to.*

If she could just—

The corridor suddenly branched off to the left.

Alicia stopped.

Take the branch, or go straight?

She tried to remember. Had she made a turn

here? Or had she just followed the corridor around?

She wasn't sure.

Come on, girl. Which way? Turn or straight?

Her mind was a blank.

Think!

Panic gripped her. Her brain seemed to have frozen.

Oh God oh God—

Her heart was drumming. She strained to remember.

Did I turn or didn't I?

She couldn't remember.

Clock's ticking. One way or the other! Don't just stand here!

Alicia went straight.

The corridor curved left, then sharply right. There were fewer rooms now. Most doors were closed.

Alicia slowed down. This part of the corridor didn't look familiar.

Did I go the wrong way?

She kept walking until she saw a large black panel along one wall. She stopped. The panel had dozens of symbols and many rows of tiny glowing lights.

She had no idea what the panel was for. But she knew for sure that she'd never seen it before.

She spun around and started to rush back in the other direction.

And then, ten steps ahead of her, a door opened.

Alicia stopped dead.

She heard voices.

She backed up until the curve in the corridor hid her from view. She pressed her back to the wall.

The door closed again.

Alicia leaned forward just enough to peek down the corridor. She saw two creatures walking. Adults.

She yanked her head back. The creatures were going the other way. But their rear eyes could easily spot her.

Alicia waited. Losing this precious time was agony. But she had no choice.

Slowly, she began to follow. She stayed well back, careful to keep out of sight. She could hear their clicks and hisses in the corridor ahead of her.

Then, another sound. From behind her.

She whirled around, saw nothing.

She waited, listened.

More voices. Were other aliens approaching from behind?

She moved ahead as quickly as she dared. The two creatures in front of her were almost at the branch-off.

Would they turn or keep walking straight?

Go straight, Alicia silently begged. *Please, just go straight.*

She heard clicks and hisses from the corridor behind her.

At least two more creatures. Maybe more.

She passed a room with a closed door. She thought about hiding. But what if the room was filled with aliens? She couldn't chance it. She walked on.

At the branch-off, the two creatures paused.

Alicia stopped, out of sight.

She waited.

If the creatures behind her caught up now, she was trapped.

The seconds inched by.

Alicia waited.

Every minute was an hour.

What if the two creatures split up? she suddenly thought.

But they didn't. After a moment, the pair continued walking. Straight ahead.

Alicia said a silent prayer of thanks. She waited until the creatures were far enough ahead. Then she dashed around the corner and down the other corridor.

There were many rooms along this corridor. But Alicia could no longer worry about whether they might be occupied. There was just no more time.

She was running now. Flying past open doorways.

Once or twice she thought she caught a glimpse of movement. But she didn't stop.

She rounded a corner and slowed down.

She remembered this section of the corridor. All the rooms were the same small size. And outside every room, beside the doorway, were circles containing symbols.

This is it. This is where I started.

She looked into one of the rooms.

Square. Empty. Yellow light.

She had arrived in a room just like this. Except the light in her room had been pale blue, not yellow.

She glanced up at the ceiling. There were the tiny patterns that she had wondered about. The ones that looked like wires or printed circuits.

Yes. She was sure. The doorway of light in Jackson field had taken her to one of these rooms.

And from these rooms, she could travel back again.

The thought made Alicia want to laugh and cry and shout all at the same time.

But which room? The wrong one might take somewhere other than Jackson field.

Africa. China. Anywhere.

She didn't care. Anywhere on Earth was better than—

An awful thought stopped her cold.

Could the wrong room take her to the creatures' own planet?

Just the idea made her dizzy with fear.

Alicia ran to the next room, looked inside.

This room was bathed in green light.

She tried another room.

The light in this one was violet.

She checked a room across the corridor.

Orange light.

Alicia's heart raced. Clearly, the different colors meant something. She guessed they had to do with target area.

She paused, looked down the corridor. She tried to think back . . . to remember where she'd arrived. She had walked out of the room and turned left. She'd passed some empty rooms . . .

Alicia moved down the corridor, trying to recall. Yes . . . . I was walking along here . . . .

She looked into another room.

It was exactly the same as the others.

Except for the light.

Blue light.

The same pale blue she remembered.

Yes!

She stepped in and glanced around.

She frowned. No control panel. Alicia remembered the symbols outside, on the wall beside the doorway.

Those were the controls. There was no control panel inside the room.

Instantly, any joy she had felt was gone.

What if someone has to be on the outside working the controls? What if I can't do it alone?

But there was no use worrying about it. She had to try.

She stepped into the corridor and studied the circles on the wall. There were at least a dozen. Each contained a different symbol. She had no time to translate them all. But if she could figure out the basics . . .

Alicia raised the word screen and started matching symbols. A few she found quickly. Others took longer. She stopped when she'd decoded six of them: *Door, Receive, Auto, Send, Monitor, Delay.* Did she have enough to work the device?

Door seemed obvious. So did *Receive* and *Send.* She wasn't sure about the others. Maybe—

Sounds in the corridor.

Alicia couldn't tell from which direction or how close.

No more time to think. It's now or never.

She touched the *Send* symbol and jumped into the room.

She waited.

Nothing happened.

Have to shut the door.

She looked for some way to close the sliding panel from inside. There was none.

She leaned outside, touched the *Door* symbol, and quickly sprang back.

The door slid closed.

Still nothing happened.

This was what she'd feared. The door was meant to be closed from outside. And unless it was shut first, Alicia guessed that the device would not accept any commands.

She touched the one symbol on the inside of the door. The panel opened again. Alicia stepped back out and stared at the symbols on the wall.

She could hear hisses and clicks. They were getting louder.

She wanted to run. But she knew there was nowhere to go.

There's got to be a way . . . .

Alicia forced herself to concentrate. To ignore her pounding heart and *think.*

They use these devices for transport. To move people, things. And probably not just to and from Earth. Surely they would have built in a way for just one creature to—

The *Delay* symbol. Maybe that was it.

Maybe the *Delay* command would let someone set the device and get in.

Alicia touched the *Delay.* The blue light inside the small room began to flash. She touched the *Door* symbol.

This time the door did not slide closed at once. The blue light kept flashing for several more seconds. Then the door shut.

Yes. *Delay* would hold the door. But would the device accept another command?

Only one way to find out. Alicia touched *Door* again. The door opened. She was reaching for *Delay* when she heard a snarl.

She glanced down the corridor.

Dal.

He was rounding the corner. Leddu was with him.

Alicia let out a cry. She poked the *Delay* symbol. The blue light started to flash. Quickly she hit *Door,* then *Send.* She jumped into the room.

She heard the creatures' hisses and clicks getting louder. If this didn't work, she was finished.

Please please please

Any second they'd be upon her. Their footsteps were right outsi—

The door closed.

The flashing stopped.

Alicia heard a faint whistling sound.

Chapter 39

Debra got up from the rock on which she and Ryan were perched. She clicked on her flashlight and swung it around. The thin beam of light barely pierced the dark.

Jackson Field was still.

"Anything?" Ryan asked.

"Just ghosts," Debra muttered. It was past 11:30. The long wait had lowered her spirits.

Ryan, too, saw little reason to feel hopeful.

"It's getting cold," he said. He rubbed his hands together.

"Cold and creepy. This place is like a cemetery at night."

"Yeah." Ryan stood up. "Guess we may as well go."

"I suppose so. It doesn't—" She stopped.

"Doesn't what?" Ryan asked.

"Shhh. Did you hear something?"

Ryan listened. "No."

Debra waited another moment. Then she shook her head.

"I guess not. Let's go."

Ryan switched on his flashlight. They started walking.

Suddenly, twenty yards to their right, there was a silent explosion of light.

Debra cried out, twisting away from the glare.

Ryan covered his eyes. He tried to look. But he was blinded.

"What *is* that?" Debra said, squinting. A large rectangle of light seemed to be shining up from the ground.

Ryan tried again to look. The intense brightness hurt his eyes.

"I don't kn—"

He stopped.

A small figure appeared directly in front of the light. It seemed to have four legs.

"Deb? You see that?"

She shielded her eyes, trying to get a better look.

"What . . . is it?"

The figure slowly rose. It swayed from side to side.

Debra gasped. "It's a person!"

The figure took a few steps, then halted. Its legs seemed unsteady.

Despite the painful light, Ryan studied the form.

"Deb . . . is that . . ."

Debra was staring, too. She saw long hair, a slim female shape.

"My Lord," she said. "I think it is."

Together, they started toward her.

Alicia blinked several times. Her legs felt weak. She looked around. Everything was blurry.

I'm outside.

The thought cut through the thick fog that filled her brain.

She felt cool air. Smelled damp soil, grass. Good smells. *Familiar* smells.

Am I . . . back? She was afraid to hope.

Slowly, her surroundings came into focus. She tried to make sense of them.

Two figures were approaching.

Oh no—

A cold wave of fear hit her. She staggered back, stopped. The doorway of light was close behind her. She glanced to one side, then the other.

Which way should I run?

"Alicia?"

The voice stopped her.

The voice, and the sound of her own name.

She stared at the two figures.

They were human.

"Alicia?" Debra said again, softly.

Alicia looked from one to the other. She couldn't believe what she was seeing.

"Am . . . am I . . . ."

Debra reached a hand out toward her. Alicia flinched.

"It's okay, Alicia. It's me. Deb."

Ryan gently touched her shoulder. "Are you all right?"

She looked at him, at Debra.

"Oh God . . . it's true." Alicia's eyes filled with tears. "It's really true . . . ."

The next second, the three of them were hugging. Alicia was sobbing.

"What happened?" Debra asked after a moment. But Alicia just shook her head. She couldn't speak yet.

Debra and Ryan exchanged glances. They felt equally relieved to have Alicia back. And equally puzzled.

"What happened?" Debra asked again.

This time, Alicia looked at her friend and tried to answer. But as soon as she saw those familiar, comforting eyes, Alicia started crying all over again.

Deb pulled her close and wrapped her arms around her. She was crying too, now.

"Will you stop, girl. You got me doing it now."

"Oh, Deb. You don't know. You just don't know." She hugged her friend tightly.

They stayed that way until Debra gently pulled away. "I think we should get out of here. Before this light makes us all blind."

Alicia nodded. "I want to go—" She broke off. Her eyes widened.

"What's the matter?" Debra asked.

Alicia was staring at Ryan. He was standing stiffly to one side. There was an odd look on his face.

A look of confusion.

And fear.

"Ryan?" Alicia said, her voice shaky.

Ryan met her eyes. He opened his mouth to speak.

No sound came out.

"Oh God. Ryan?"

"You okay, Ryan?" Debra asked. She was concerned. He suddenly looked awful. She hoped he wasn't having a heart attack.

Ryan's head twitched several times.

He took a step toward Alicia.

He tried again to speak, but couldn't. His eyes were wide. He looked terrified.

Alicia had seen this expression before.

She had seen it on Yonte's viewer.

"Ryan! Can you hear me?" Alicia shouted.

Debra looked at her. She heard panic in her friend's voice.

"Alicia, what is it? What's going on?"

Ryan took another step toward Alicia. His body shuddered.

Suddenly, one hand shot out and fastened on Alicia's wrist.

"Ryan, no!" she cried.

Debra grabbed Ryan's arm. "What're you doing? Let her go. Have you lost your mind? You're hurting her."

Ryan's free hand locked on Alicia's other arm. Alicia screamed. She tried to pull away.

Ryan's fingers tightened. His grip was like iron.

Debra was pulling on Ryan, shouting at him to let go.

But Ryan seemed not to hear. He moved forward, forcing Alicia back.

Toward the light.

Alicia shrieked and tried to dig in her heels. She pushed back, threw her weight against him. But he was like a machine.

"No, Ryan! No!"

He pushed her backwards another step. Her back was almost at the doorway of light.

Alicia twisted and struggled. She brought a knee up into Ryan's middle. Once, twice.

His grip only grew tighter.

Debra had one arm around his neck, choking him. With her other hand, she was punching and clawing at his head.

Ryan still moved forward.

"Try to fight, Ryan," Alicia pleaded. "You have to try!"

Ryan began shaking, violently, like a sick man racked by fever chills. Alicia looked into his eyes and saw utter horror.

"Please, Ryan, fight! If you send me back, I'm dead!"

They were beside the doorway now. The light was blinding.

Alicia pushed back with all her strength. Debra pulled and punched and scratched.

Blood ran from Ryan's nose and down his cheeks. His face and neck were red and bruised.

But he seemed to feel none of it.

Only his eyes showed any pain.

Abruptly, his body tensed. He pulled Alicia toward him. She felt his arms trembling.

"Fight, Ryan! Fight!"

Ryan's head began to jerk wildly from side to side. He gasped for breath. His whole body vibrated. His face shone with sweat.

Then, suddenly, his mouth opened wide in a soundless scream. He staggered. His head fell back. His hold on Alicia loosened.

And he crumpled to the ground.

Alicia dropped to her knees beside him.

"Ryan!"

Except for red scratches and smears of blood, his face was colorless. His eyes were closed.

"Ryan, can you hear me?"

Debra knelt down next to Alicia. She looked grim.

Ryan's eyes remained shut, but his lips were moving. Alicia leaned close.

"Hurts . . ." The word was barely a whisper.

Alicia glanced at Debra. "We have to get help," she said, tears running down both cheeks.

Debra stood up. "You stay with him. I'll go."

Alicia nodded, and Debra left.

A moment later, the light went out.

The doorway had closed.

Epilogue

In the assembly room, Turfim was reporting on the Earth Project. Turfim was chief scientist. He was in charge of the Implant research group. He had replaced Hukolf eleven years ago.

More than ninety adults and twenty learners filled the large room. All listened intently to Turfim's words. When he finished, the scientist turned to the Three for questions.

Nemm spoke first. She was now the oldest of the Three.

"We are pleased, Turfim. Your group has made significant progress."

Povden spoke next. He had taken Dal's place.

"Will you review for us the success rate?" he asked.

"Over 91 percent total success," Turfim said proudly. "About 5 percent partial success. Only 4 percent failure or loss."

The room buzzed loudly. These were the best numbers yet. Even better than expected.

"Excellent," Povden said. "Truly excellent."

The third member of the Three leaned forward in his chair. He was the youngest and newest member. But he was well known. He sat in the chair that had once been his father's.

"Your group has done fine work," Yonte said. He had grown to full adult height over the years. His voice had deepened. "These numbers are outstanding. But tell us exactly, what percent loss?"

Turfim did not hesitate. He knew Yonte would ask.

"Less than two percent."

Yonte glanced to the side of the room, where the learners sat. They were all listening closely, as he himself had done when he had been a learner.

"Fewer than two of one hundred subjects die?" Yonte asked.

"Correct," Turfim said.

Yonte thought of the Earth female, as he so often had over the years. He had promised himself to try to spare as many of her people as possible. Turfim had successfully cut the loss rate to a fraction of what it had been.

"A great improvement," he told the scientist.

Turfim acknowledged the compliment and walked back to his seat.

What would the Earth female think? Yonte wondered. Surely she would see that, by waiting, they had shown compassion. Surely she would agree that they had done all they could. That he had done all he could.

Postponing action against Earth for so many years had caused much debate. Few voices in the assembly room expressed great concern for Earth's inhabitants. Indeed, some had called for their elimination.

Yet, Leddu, like his son after him, had always urged patience. There was little to be gained by rushing into action, he said many times. Better to let the scientists continue with their work. Nemm had agreed.

Dal, however, had not. While some confessed grudging respect for the Earth female's resourcefulness, Dal felt only annoyance. The alien's escape had made him more impatient than ever.

Not until Povden took Dal's place was the matter finally settled. Like Leddu and Nemm, Povden saw no reason for haste. The Three agreed to give the scientists more time.

Yonte knew the outcome would have been different had the Earth female been able to rouse her people to action. But, just as Leddu had predicted, her efforts were in vain. When she spoke of four-armed aliens plotting against Earth, people reacted with disbelief, even laughter. They had heard too many tales of flying saucers and men from Mars to take them seriously.

How ironic, Yonte thought, that this disbelief had saved her life. Dal had wanted to pursue and destroy her. But even Dal had to agree that doing so would only arouse suspicion. Watch and wait, Leddu advised. The Earth female's story will fade away. Her claims will be dismissed as a teenager's ramblings. And, as time passed, Leddu had been proven right.

Now, as audience members talked quietly among themselves, the Three conferred. The subject of discussion was the same throughout the assembly room: Turfim's report.

Finally, Nemm rose. She stepped forward, and the room fell silent.

"At long last, the moment is at hand," she said. "We will make final preparations for the Earth Project."

The audience buzzed loudly with approval.

"Agreed," said Povden, rising to stand beside her.

Yonte thought once more of the Earth female. When the time came, she alone, of all those on her planet, would understand what was happening. Would this knowledge lessen her fear, he wondered, or add to it? He did not know.

Yonte rose slowly from his chair. Of those present, only he could say that he had known an Earth being. Perhaps this was why he hesitated before coming forward to stand with Povden and Nemm.

He glanced around the room. Everyone clearly was pleased with Nemm's announcement.

"Agreed," Yonte said.